PROMISE

THE NARAVAN CHRONICLES 1

ISABO KELLY

T&D PUBLISHING

PROMISE

Published 2018 by T&D Publishing
Cover design: © 2017 EJR Digital Art
Interior book design © 2018 T&D Publishing
ISBN-13: 978-1-944600-10-5 (Trade Paperback Edition)

This is a work of fiction. All of the characters, places, organizations, and
events portrayed are either products of the author's imagination or are used
fictitiously. Any resemblance to actual persons, living or dead, business
establishments, events, or locales is entirely coincidental.

First printing T&D Publishing edition: March 2018
For information, contact T&D Publishing www.tanddpublishing.com

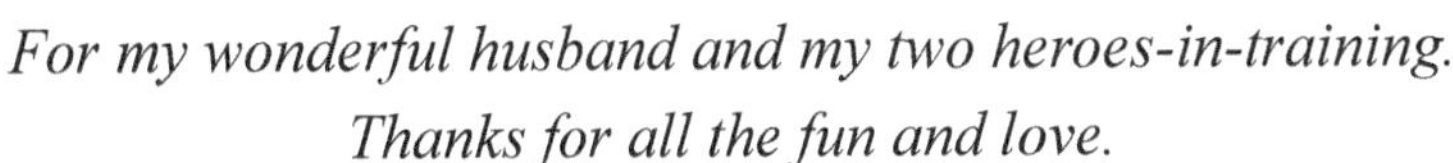

For my wonderful husband and my two heroes-in-training. Thanks for all the fun and love.

For my parents and my sister for their constant support and belief.

And for Kem and Peter for helping me name things in this book way back when it was just a work-in-progress.

CHAPTER ONE

I'VE ALWAYS WONDERED WHAT I WOULD DO IF THERE CAME A time to stand against society, to stand for something…something important. Something that mattered. Would I have the courage to fight for a belief? To defend an ideal with my very life? To kill for a cause?

That last has always been the hardest question for me to answer. In my imagination, my life is easier to give away than the taking of another life. But that's in theory.

Who knows what we might do in practice?

—From the journal of Kira Farseaker

"KIRA?"

"Hush," Kira hissed over her shoulder, never taking her eyes from the roadblock ahead. "Keep your heads about you," she told the four women in the back of the van. "They can't know if you don't give us away."

Kira studied the stiff navy uniforms of the Guards, her practiced eye hunting for the familiar face. He was there. She knew he would be there somewhere. This blockade had his mark.

Convulsively her hands clenched the rough steering wheel. By force of will, she relaxed both her grip and her shoulders. He wouldn't break her. Not now. And he wouldn't find her out.

They inched forward in the long line of vehicles, most the latest in synthesized transport—clean, efficient, small and cheap—toward the handful of Guards at the roadside. The day was bright with late autumn sun reflecting off the cars and the tarmac paving of the road, glittering in the rust sand that peeked between the long, low buildings edging this side of the city. Beyond the buildings, the land was covered with a mix of palms, succulent shrubs and sparse, patchy salt grass. At this southern edge, the faintest hint of sea scent wafted in the breeze.

This was the kind of day Kira loved as a child. Warm, but with a hint of winter to come. Days for playing in the backyard or running on the beach with her father. Now, she barely noted the sparse clouds scuttling across the azure sky or the late autumn flowers that still purpled the white salt grass. Her attention was focused entirely on the roadblock ahead, searching the Guards for that too-familiar face.

Seemingly at random, the Guard on the left signaled and sent vehicles off to a side area, near a hastily erected portable office, for closer inspection. Kira watched as the passengers exited their vehicles at a hand gesture from one Guard and stepped over to a second group of Guards who were obviously asking questions. Although she couldn't hear the interrogations, she'd been subjected to such "standard inquiries" before and knew exactly what was happening.

Kira felt her lip curl in a snarl. All very efficient. All very organized and outwardly by the book. She forced her mouth back to a straight, expressionless line.

Ten years ago, she wouldn't have been bothered by this scene. It was routine. The Guards were free to randomly inspect the citizens of Narava for contraband, drugs, illegal goods, interplanetary imports, immigrants trying to avoid taxes and fees, aliens. The Shifters.

No. Ten years ago, she wouldn't have been bothered. Because ten years ago there was so much she didn't know.

They reached the forward Guard, and Kira prepared for the inevitable questions. She didn't bother to smile or flirt. The Guard, a man in his late fifties, wore the familiar signet on his uniform. He already knew who she was.

"Farseaker," he greeted without inflection. His gaze traveled over her face, then into the back of the van, taking in the four other women.

"Officer Herot," Kira returned. She didn't know the man, not well, but she'd seen him before, dealt with him before.

"You know the drill, Farseaker. Contraband? Illegals?"

She couldn't help the cynical smile that answered his questions. He already knew her answers. "What do you think, Officer?"

"I think you've been skirting the law for too long now, Farseaker. He knows you're involved with them."

"If he had any proof that I was involved in something illegal," she said evenly, "he'd have had me locked away in a hole a very long time ago, Herot. And he would relish putting me there."

The Guard's thick dark brows drew together over a prominent nose. His thin lips pursed for an instant, then flattened. "Pull the van over to the side," he said, gesturing to the second set of Guards. "They'll have to be questioned further." He nodded to the four in the back. "And the van will be inspected."

"Of course." Kira didn't argue. She pulled the van to the side, hissing another silencing order as a nervous chatter started behind her. "Remember," she said under her breath, "they don't know anything. Can't know anything. Just keep your heads and we'll be all right."

"Kira?"

She looked over her shoulder at the sound of the timid voice. Vettine was only nineteen years old. Her cropped blonde hair and heart-shaped face gave her an ethereal beauty, but her deep jade eyes were wide with fear, making her appear every year of her youth. "You'll be okay," Kira assured her with a firm voice. "Don't panic on me now."

The girl took a long, shaky breath, straightened her shoulders and nodded.

"Good girl," Kira murmured as a Guard walked up to the passenger side of the van. This Guard was a man she'd never seen before. He was young, but not too young. Mid-thirties, she guessed at a glance. Handsome, but far from pretty. A faint scar along his right jaw and the first few wrinkles of his age saw to that. His short, brown hair held just a touch of wave. His black-coffee eyes were hard and efficient. But there was something…

Something in his eyes. Something familiar, that she couldn't name. Maybe it was an underlying quality of pain, or the hint of humanity she so rarely found in the Guard. Whatever it was, it was absent from the firm line of his mouth, the set of his jaw, the sharp movement of his arm as he gestured the four women behind her out of the van's side door. Whatever it was, he hid it well.

When Kira turned to open her door, he stopped her. "You're to wait in the car, ma'am."

And she almost smiled. He had a beautiful, husky voice. A voice she wouldn't mind hearing more. Her stomach twisted just a little, pleasantly reminding her that she was still a woman. Her gaze dropped to his chest, a rather nice, broad one she thought before noticing the signet above his left breast.

Her self-control snapped back into place.

She faced forward, watching through the front windshield of the van as a half-dozen fully armed soldiers led her four friends a short distance away. She tried to relax against the seat, tried to ignore the inconvenient tear in the imitation leather that poked her in the back. This could take hours if Ennoren saw fit to detain them.

The sound of the passenger door opening startled her. She turned to see the Guard settle himself onto the floorboard, shifting so that he wasn't visible above the dash. Kira cocked her head to one side, raising her eyebrows, and the man flashed the most charming smile she'd ever seen. The grin was just a touch guilty and would have made him seem like a mischievous boy if it hadn't stretched the scar and deepened the wrinkles around his eyes.

He plucked a pack of cigarettes from a pocket inside his uniform jacket and showed them to her.

"Not allowed to smoke on duty." He tapped one cigarette free, stuck it in his mouth, then returned the rest to his pocket and pulled out a small lighter. Before he lit up, he extended a hand. "David."

"Kira." She shook his hand, quick and firm, and pulled back before she had time to notice how nice his grip felt.

He lit the cigarette, took a long drag, then offered the end to her. She stared at the thing for a moment before helping herself to a puff. Through the cloud of tobacco-scented smoke she exhaled, she studied him. "You been with the Guard long?" she asked, handing the cigarette back.

"Twelve years now." He took another drag, never taking his gaze from her face.

"You're one of Ennoren's." She wasn't asking. She knew the signet on his uniform too well.

He nodded, his dark eyes still locked to hers. "For about three years."

She half-smiled, chuckled and shook her head. "Too bad, really." She turned to see how her friends were doing.

All four seemed to be holding up under the scrutiny of the men questioning them. Vettine's shoulders were straight, her posture unwavering. Grainne's stance was relaxed and cocky as she tossed her waist-length red hair over one shoulder. Breeanne had her arms crossed over her chest, her legs braced slightly apart. Her pale skin was flushed, but her expression controlled. And Jo, with her stylishly braided black hair brushing her shoulders in the breeze, had her hands on her hips, a slight smile on her full mouth and a sexy glint in her violet eyes. Kira couldn't help smiling. Her second would flirt with the Devil himself if she were standing at the gates of Hell.

"Why too bad?"

The husky voice brought her attention back to the man sitting on the floorboard of her van. He offered her the cigarette again, and she took a long drag before answering. "I would have liked to get to know you. Under better circumstances. I think I could have liked you," she answered without guile, a slight, sad smile tugging at her mouth.

"Could have?"

She shrugged. "You're one of Ennoren's men." She faced forward again because there was really no need for further explanation.

"You're jumping to conclusions. Judging me based on the commander I work under. You don't know me."

Kira snorted and met his gaze. "It doesn't matter whether I know you or not. You work for Ennoren."

A movement to her left caught her attention, and she turned away from David's narrowed eyes. She reached down for the cigarette without taking her eyes off the man walking toward the van. When she'd taken another drag, she said, "Your boss is on his way over. Better let me finish this."

David slid out of the van, unhooked a thin, foot-long cylindrical device from his belt and began running it over the interior of the van without another word. Her gaze flicked to the device, then back to the approaching commander. The steady beep of the detector echoed in Kira's pulse as she watched Ennoren step up to her open window.

He was tall and thin, with a face Kira had once found

interesting, if not attractive. All lines and angles, sharp nose, hard mouth, heavy-lidded blue eyes; his face was imposing, commanding and often intimidating. But Kira had long since stopped being intimidated by Ennoren.

He looked at the cigarette in her hand, then into her eyes. "I thought you didn't smoke."

She set the cigarette against her lips, inhaled deeply and blew smoke in his face. "I don't."

He waved the smoke away, a sneer forming in place of a smile. For a long moment he studied her, his gaze running over her faded, ripped jeans and cotton flannel shirt. Then he turned to study her van, pointedly staring at the cracked dash, battered steering wheel and worn imitation leather upholstery. "New van?"

Kira nodded.

"I didn't think you'd be into this late twentieth-century Earth fad." He frowned. "But then, you always were a fashionable socialite, weren't you? And since you have the money to afford this mock-up of an Earth car…" He let the sentence trail off as he held her gaze. "You're looking good, Kira."

She returned his stare, taking another pull on the cigarette so she didn't have to answer.

When she remained silent, Ennoren shifted his attention to David. "Find anything, Officer Cario?"

David snapped to attention. "No, sir. Appears clean."

"Well," Ennoren said, turning a contemptuous glare on Kira, "appearances can lie."

"Was that a dig, Eain?" Kira kept her tone mild, even as she used his first name in front of another Guard—something she did only to annoy him. His mother had been a poet and fond of alliteration. Ennoren went out of his way to keep his full name, Eain Edward Evander Ennoren, from his subordinates.

He covered his indignation well, but the slight narrowing of his eyes and the flare of his nostrils gave him away. "Take from it what you will." He paused, studying her again. When he spoke, his voice was low. "The ring will collapse out from under you, Kira. It won't be long now. Do you know what will happen to you when you're found guilty of treason and conspiracy to commit treason against the planetary government?"

"They'll throw me into a hole?"

"They'll throw you into space without a suit," he hissed. Dropping his voice again, he leaned into the car, putting his face only inches from hers. "End this now, Kira. End it. Tell me where they hide. I'll make sure you get off with a light sentence." A slight smile curled his lips. "I might even arrange to serve as your paroler. Just like old times, eh?"

Kira turned her head to take one final puff off the cigarette, giving herself time to gain control over both her revulsion and her anger, before confronting his leer. "There's a reason those times are old, Eain. I wouldn't have gone to all the trouble of divorcing you if I'd wanted to end up right back under your thumb. Besides—" she half-smiled, half-snarled at him, "—how would I know where they hide?"

She watched with satisfaction as his leer transformed into a lip-trembling scowl. Flicking the cigarette past his shoulder, she turned back to David. He was standing at attention, a silent, emotionless witness to the scene. "Forgive my ex. He seems to think I'm some sort of underground anti-government terrorist leader."

David raised an eyebrow. "Are you?"

She smiled. Then she laughed.

The side door to the van opened and her friends climbed up to the padded bench along the side of the van. Kira kept her gaze on David, enjoying the twinkle of amusement in his eyes that didn't filter into any other part of his expression. When the side door slammed into place, she leaned across the passenger seat and pulled that door shut.

"It really is too bad we didn't meet under different circumstances, officer," she said when David leaned into the open window.

His crooked grin made his scar jump. His knowing stare set her pulse dancing. She chuckled and moved back behind the wheel. Without another glance at her ex-husband, she put the van into gear and returned to the line of traffic hurrying away from the blockade.

DAVID WATCHED HER GO, feeling like he'd been kicked in the gut and strangely liking the sensation. Kira was interesting. Beautiful, yes. Enough so that his pulse sped just remembering her golden brown eyes and the sound of her sultry chuckle. But there was something else about her, under that smile and sharp attitude, that he wanted to get to know better. Something that was almost familiar.

He couldn't remember the last time a woman had caught his attention, or his lust, this way. He wasn't even sure if another woman had before, and that was pretty damned terrifying. But anyone who could make Commander Ennoren lose control was worth getting to know. Whether she scared David or not, Ennoren's ex-wife could prove to be quite valuable.

His heart stopped for a single beat when the commander cleared his throat from right beside him. Out of the corner of his eye, David saw Ennoren staring after the rapidly retreating van too.

"Don't let her pretty face fool you, Officer Cario," Ennoren said, his voice low, almost a whisper. "She's not as sweet as she appears. A viper lives beneath that silky skin."

Knowing it best to keep his opinions to himself, David studied his commander's profile. His nostrils flared, but other than that, his sharp features were now composed and emotionless. Before David could look away, Ennoren turned, catching and holding his gaze.

"You don't believe me?"

"I have no opinion on the matter, Commander."

Ennoren smiled. "Yes, you do."

He cocked his head to one side, watching David with a sharp, perceptive gaze. The stare was disconcerting, but David had hidden from it before.

"Doesn't matter," the commander finally said. "Because I think I can use this situation to our benefit." He turned toward the temporary command post. "In my office, Cario," Ennoren ordered. "We've got a few things to discuss."

***

KIRA PULLED past the front of her house and into a narrow lane at the edge of her property. The paved road was flanked by thick stone walls covered in ivy and overhung by rows of dense, leafy trees. The entrance was so overgrown by foliage, it was almost impossible to see unless you knew where to look. The driveway led to the family garage, and only Kira used it now. Visitors used the front drive. Friends had other ways to get in.

As a child, she'd thought the lane, with its cover and solitude, a silly addition to the estate. But her father had liked his privacy, coveting it more and more as the years went by. She hadn't understood that need. Why should people want to hide behind walls? But then, she'd been an open and curious child who'd grown into a guileless adult.

Until her father's death.

She stopped the van halfway up the drive, puffing out a breath. She didn't have time to dwell on all the changes in her life. There was still too much to do. She opened her door and followed the others to stand a few paces in front of the van.

The transformation never ceased to amaze Kira. One moment, a perfectly ordinary van sat in the lane. The next, a beautiful, iridescent, hairless creature stood staring at them. Its huge, multifaceted eyes whirled through purple to blue to green as it tilted its otherwise featureless head to one side. The long lines of neck and limbs made the creature appear taller and far thinner than it actually was, but since it could shift to most any shape, its body dimensions were relative.

"That was close."

Kira smiled at its whispery voice floating through her mind. No matter their emotional state, the Shifters' voices always sounded quiet to her. *"Not as close as that, Xep. He never suspected."*

A human-like mouth formed in the iridescent gold skin of

Xep's face. The mouth turned up in a mocking smile. Though they did have a form of external hearing, Shifters had no natural mouths or vocal cords. They could only speak using telepathy when in their natural state. And only a very few humans could hear and speak back in the same manner. But Xep was fond of shifting just enough to convey all too human facial expressions.

"He suspects, Kira," the Shifter said as the mouth melted away.

"But he doesn't suspect this. He doesn't have a clue Shifters like you exist."

Jo reached behind a thick clump of ivy and tapped a code into a hidden panel, opening a disguised passage in the stone wall leading to the interior of Kira's estate. The group ducked through the overhanging ivy and the door closed silently behind them. They walked over short, spongy green grass to a second secret hatch in the ground. This time, using her foot, Vettine tapped out the code that opened the door. After a short pause, a section of grass slid over with a hiss of escaping air. All six dropped down the ladder into a steel-lined tunnel, and Kira punched in the code at a command panel to seal the hatch again.

They turned and walked down the tunnel, lights overhead flicking on as they approached, flicking off once they passed.

"Kira." Xep's quiet voice touched her mind. *"It will not be long before he discovers. Ennoren is a smart man. A cunning human. And he is vicious."*

She nodded, silently considering Xep's words. She knew Ennoren was vicious, had seen it firsthand. Had run away from it in disgust and anger. And she knew he was clever. But she was clever, too.

"We're almost ready, Xep. We can hide from him until then." She glanced at the Shifter walking beside her, hoping to catch some sign of emotion in a face she couldn't read unless it allowed her. *"This won't be easy."*

"Nothing has been easy since the humans first came here."

Though no emotion came across in its mind-speak, Kira imagined the bitterness associated with that statement, and it made her heart hurt. She closed off her emotional response forcefully and turned her attention to the tunnel. She couldn't change what had been done to the Shifters in the past, and she couldn't save all of them now. But she could sure as hell try to save some of them.

"He seemed very nice."

Xep's quick subject change caught Kira so by surprise, she stopped for an instant. The odd looks the other women gave her started her moving again with an embarrassed grimace.

"Ennoren?" she asked.

"Officer David Cario. He seemed very nice."

The mention of the handsome officer's name brought with it an image of coffee-colored eyes, thick, dark hair and a dancing scar. Her stomach clenched and a tingle spread over her thighs at the memory of his smile. It had been much too long since she'd last been with a man, she thought ruefully.

"He's one of Ennoren's," she told Xep, forcing her mind-speak to sound stern. *"It doesn't matter if he's the nicest man on Narava."*

"He was quite taken with you. And you with him."

"And you're an expert on the subject, are you, Xep?" Her

irritation leaked through with the comment. *"How would you know, anyway?"*

She glanced at the Shifter. The mouth that had formed in its face was grinning. She snorted and turned away, hoping Xep hadn't seen her blush.

"Stuff it," she muttered aloud at it. If she hadn't known better, she would have sworn the Shifter laughed.

CHAPTER TWO

I MET THE PERFECT MAN LAST NIGHT. HE'S A CAPTAIN IN THE Guards, very serious and confident. Not exactly handsome, but he's got an interesting face. And the best part is, my father hates him!

I can't wait to see him again. His name is Eian. Captain Eian Ennoren.

—From the journal of Kira Farseaker

KIRA STOOD at the edge of the elaborately carved red stone bridge, trying to slow her thumping heartbeat. The public transport line stopped just at the edge of the Grand Bridge. She was the only one who'd gotten off. No government-funded transport dared cross that bridge. Visitors were left to walk into the Docks at their own risk.

She'd crossed that bridge before, walked the gray flagstone streets of a city built above the Dreic Sea and supported by wooden pillars sunk into the sediment below. She'd even dealt with some of the less than lawful citizens of the Docks. But always during the day.

Night settled over the area, dark and forbidding. The moons had yet to rise, leaving only the stars and the glow from the city to light the bridge. She hesitated for a moment more. But she couldn't back out now. Squaring her shoulders and straightening her cropped jacket, Kira stepped onto the bridge.

"Do you think that's a good idea?"

The unexpected voice made her gut clench and her hands shake for just an instant. She fisted her left hand, letting her short nails bite into the flesh of her palm. When she turned to face the stranger cautioning her, she was in control again.

Recognizing the face made her grin and relax her hand; then her smile dropped to a suspicious frown. "What are you doing here?"

David stepped from the shadows across the road and strode toward her. He wasn't in uniform, but there was still a formality to the way he wore his loose black pants and tight turtleneck shirt. His black leather jacket was a nod to the current fashion fad, but it looked too new and clean.

"I should ask you the same question," he said in that smoky voice she found so toe-curling. "This place isn't safe at night." His dark gaze lingered on her red mini-dress and calf-high boots.

"I've been here before." She raised her chin, flashing him a small smirk. "And this isn't exactly a place where the Guards are welcome."

"I'm not on duty tonight. And we're not forbidden entrance."

"That still doesn't explain why you're here."

"Maybe I'm looking for something…hard to obtain."

Kira narrowed her eyes. The Docks were notorious for providing things hard to obtain. The city was run by a family of very powerful and very dangerous criminals. The government called them a mafia. They bought and sold illegals, smuggled goods and people, ran gaming and prostitution rings, auctioned slaves, both alien and human, pandered to the drugs and technology trades, and all in the open streets and canals of the Docks.

The Guard didn't go into the city—officially.

Government propaganda had it that the encroachment of the law into the well-established city would only start a bloody, vicious war. As long as the criminal element remained localized in the Docks, they were no danger to the citizenry. Common gossip vouched that the mafia paid high-placed officials well to keep the law out of the city. Common gossip also held that the mafia possessed certain alliances and weapons that scared even the "all-powerful" planetary government.

"I wouldn't have taken you for a Docks patron," Kira said at last, still not convinced by David's excuse.

"I wouldn't have guessed it of you, either," he countered. "I haven't heard your explanation yet."

She bristled at the underlying order. His tone came dangerously close to reminding her of her ex-husband. The man, she reminded herself, who gave this man his orders. "And I don't suspect you'll hear it anytime soon. Now, if you'll excuse me." She turned and started across the bridge, her earlier fear replaced by indignation.

David fell in step beside her. The thick sea air moved across the bridge, through the buildings, carrying with it the scent of fish and an underlying hint of something Kira couldn't name and wasn't sure she wanted to. She paused at the edge of the bridge, letting her eyes adjust to the soft orange glow of the city streets. Then she headed down the first major walkway into the heart of the Docks, trying to ignore the man that had followed her over the bridge. To her irritation, he stayed beside her.

"I imagine you have other things to do here," she snapped, stopping to stare up at him. She found it disconcerting that despite her high-heeled boots, he was still several inches taller than her. In heels, she was the same height as Ennoren, and she'd considered him a tall man. Even more disconcerting was the scent of David's cologne, a combination of musk and spice blending with the leather smell of his jacket. It managed to tease her senses without overpowering them. She wanted to lean closer to that faint smell, to fill her lungs with it.

"I'll walk you to where you're going," he said, ignoring her dismissal. They stood alone on the main street, washed in orange light. He glanced again at the miniskirt and her long length of exposed thigh. "I'm not comfortable letting you walk here alone."

Kira stared at him, her emotions shifting rapidly from amazement to anger and finally settling on amusement. She smiled. When his eyes creased suspiciously, she laughed, a sound that boomed in the quiet streets. A man in a dark bodysuit and flight jacket who'd just stepped out of an alley glanced toward them, then gave them a wide berth.

Kira forgot to be afraid or angry. She patted David on the arm and grinned. "Very gallant of you. Not necessary. But a gallant offer nonetheless. Would that I could allow it." He frowned and she hurried on. "The…hard to obtain item I've come to get is sold by a man that wouldn't take kindly to me appearing with a…bodyguard." She said the last with an upward lilt in her voice, half questioning, half teasing him with the title. "Besides, I'm sure you're not here to follow a virtual stranger around. Go about your business, Officer. I'm well able to take care of myself."

He didn't quite smile, but his scar jumped under the twitching muscle of his jaw. "As the lady wishes." He bowed from the waist, which only made her laugh more.

She walked away, enjoying the tingles he'd started in her body. When she felt his gaze still following her, she added a bit more swing to her hips. It had been a long time since a man made her feel this feminine and sexy.

She turned a corner, crossed a canal and headed down a second narrow street. Her momentary thrill at flirting with a handsome man vanished behind the need to stay alert and ready for anything. She watched the shadows as she walked through the alleys with as much attitude as she could muster. The surrounding buildings were all several stories tall, with a variety of cast-iron or stone balconies and window boxes decorating the stucco facades. In daylight, the colors varied from muted creams, corals and tans, to darker blues, purples, oranges and greens. The canals, kept cleaned by the natural currents of the Dreic, still held a faint fishy smell that permeated every alley and building in the city. The Docks had been fashioned after the Earth city of Venice in Italy. And if the pictures were anything to go on, Kira thought the Docks a pretty close replica.

She crossed a second bridge, the dark waters of the canal reflecting the orange glow of the streetlamps, and ducked down a final alley. The club's entrance wasn't easy to find. You had to know the exact door. The owners had designed it that way. She stepped up to the ordinary-looking green wood door and stared at the brass knocker. The cooling autumn breeze that managed to flow down some corridors and streets in the tightly packed city didn't reach into this particular alley. A trickle of sweat inched down her spine. Raising a hand, she hoped the information they'd bought had been worth the price.

She knocked with bare knuckles against the thick wood, a pattern that was supposed to allow entrance without question. The door opened and she came face-to-face with a very large, very hairy Binnean doorman. The Binneans were one of the few sentient alien races humans had encountered since embarking on their exploration of the galaxy. The species was known for its strength and violent tendencies. Kira held her breath and waited for the giant bouncer to comment.

When the Binnean didn't ask any questions but merely stepped aside for her to enter, she released her breath, feeling lightheaded with relief. She crossed to the long brass and glass bar which ran the length of the ground floor and took a moment to study the club, letting her eyes adjust to the smoky light.

Everything was black and gold. The marble floors, the arched ceilings, the second floor galleries, the glossy table-tops, the glow of imitation candles, even the majority of the patrons wore some variation of black and gold. No, she decided after a more thorough look. Most of the men wore some combination of black and gold. Most of the women wore bright, flamboyant colors. But there were too few women in the club to notice those flashes of color on first glance. Kira wondered at the small number of women but was glad their informant had told her to wear red.

A Binnean barman stepped over to her and asked if she wanted a drink. The creature was so wide, he would have made three human men. His thick head and body were covered with neatly combed black hair, and the only clothing he wore was a pair of loose-fitting gold woven trousers. Two large, emerald green eyes poked out of the brown, smooth skin of his face. His nose was thick and long over a straight, full-lipped mouth. Hearing a polite question from that mouth seemed at odds with the all the violent stories she'd heard of the Binneans. But then, in the Docks, business was business.

She ordered a beer and studied the booths at the rear of the club more closely. She'd been given a description, but already she'd seen a number of men who might fit. For a second, a tinge of panic churned in her stomach. What if she couldn't recognize him? What if he didn't show? What if she picked the wrong man?

She was considering taking a walk around the upper galleries when one of the men at the rear of the club caught her eye, a slight, roguish grin tipping the corners of his mouth. The shoulder-length sandy hair and light eyes, the overall build, even the pilot's black jumpsuit all matched the description of her contact. She took one final glance around the ground floor, then picked up her bottle of icy beer and walked slowly toward the man, noting his casual, arrogant slouch in the booth and his undisguised observation of her legs.

"Raf?" she asked when she stood across the table from him.

His grin crooked to one side, and he nodded for her to take a seat. "So you need a pilot and a ship?"

His blunt question surprised her. She'd thought there'd be more subtlety. At the very least, she'd expected him to make a more lecherous comment to start the conversation.

The fact that he didn't made her look at him more closely. One arm was slung across the top of the bench, the other hung loose on the seat beside him, conveniently within reach of a hip-holstered weapon. His cocky grin belied the vigilant darting of his blue eyes.

She slid into the booth. He may have looked at ease, but he was ready for anything. For some reason, that helped Kira relax. And after another careful moment's consideration, she decided she liked Raf Tygran. She didn't trust him. But she liked him.

"How much?" she asked, taking a sip of beer. She didn't flinch when he named his price. She'd expected something higher. "When?"

"I can be ready to leave planet within the week. I've a few details to settle first." His lip twitched. "But getting them onto the ship and off planet isn't gonna be easy."

Kira nodded.

When she didn't answer his unspoken question, he spoke it. "You have a plan, I take it?"

"Of course."

"What about the detector rings?"

"You worry about flying the ship." She set her half-empty

bottle on the table. "I'll worry about the detectors." And before he could ask, she said, "I'll have a clearance code as well by the time we leave."

He shrugged and reached for the nearly full glass of some orange-colored drink that sat on the table in front of him. "Your show, honey. I'm paid for my pilot skills, not my tactical skills."

"I hope you have a few tactical skills as well. Getting where we're going isn't going to be easy. And if it's suspected you've helped us, you won't be able to show your face here again."

He raised his eyebrows and grinned. "Do you think I'm able to do that comfortably now?" His gaze flicked around the room before settling on her again. "Why do you think I come here?"

Kira glanced at the room, then leveled a hard look at him. "Why do you come here? To this club, I mean?"

"Paid anonymity. You can buy just about anything in the Docks. Anonymity is more expensive than a lot of things, but not so expensive as others."

"Why are there so few women here?" She picked up her bottle and cradled it in her hands without sipping.

"Too early. Crowds build with the night."

"Doesn't it lessen your anonymity to be seen with one of the few women in the club?"

He grinned, a mixture of smug self-assurance and amusement. "I'm too handsome for anyone to question why I'd be with one of the few women here. Especially since you're quite a stunner yourself. Seems like an obvious conclusion to me."

For just an instant, she was awed by the sheer arrogance

of that statement. Then she laughed and took a drink of her beer. He really should have annoyed her, but the blatant cockiness he wore like a shirt made it impossible to take his flirtations seriously.

Unlike David's more subtle seductive manner, she thought before she could stop herself. Her stomach did a giddy dance at the memory of his scent and dark eyes. She swallowed hard and reminded herself that David worked for Ennoren. That fact wasn't going to change, no matter how he made her feel. And within the week, Kira would be leaving Narava forever. Another fact that wasn't going to change. She dropped her gaze and drank deeply from her warming bottle. A slight shiver shook her shoulders despite the relative warmth of the club.

"You okay?"

Raf's mild concern surprised her yet again. She smiled and nodded, forcing her melancholy away. There wasn't really much here for her to miss. And there was so much to gain.

"Sir—" A hesitant voice coughed from the end of the booth, startling Kira. She hadn't even heard the Binnean doorman approach the table. "A message was left for you at the door." The guard handed Raf a flat, palm-sized electronic notepad.

Raf frowned, then pressed the spot at the bottom of the screen to start the message scrolling. His frown deepened. Nodding his thanks to the doorman, the pilot waited until they were alone again before speaking.

When he looked up from the pad, all flirtation and cockiness had vanished. "I'm afraid I'll have to call the evening short. It seems my business here has come to me."

Kira raised a brow as he rose and gestured for her to proceed him from the curved seat of the booth. "Does this affect our deal?"

"No. Where can I get in touch with you?"

"Pat'll know how to find me."

He nodded, distracted, and put a hand on her lower back as he ushered her toward the door. Kira didn't resist, until she noticed a familiar face at the bar.

She stopped, suspicion warring with irritation. "David."

"Kira." His gaze flicked to Raf, who was standing just behind her with his hand firmly around her waist. "Who's your friend?" It wasn't a casual question.

"A friend," she answered evenly. "Didn't know you frequented this place." She was a little nonplussed to see how well his all-black attire fit in with the surrounding club. His manner had also changed. The formality she'd seen earlier had lapsed into a relaxed but powerful stance that dared others to mess with him. Before, he'd seemed so decent, so nice for a Guard. Now he looked dangerous.

"I don't." He still hadn't taken his gaze from the pilot standing behind her.

The bristling of male challenge was thick in the air between them, and an irritant to Kira's skin. She didn't have time for this show.

"Nice to see you again, David." She turned to face Raf, deftly removing his arm from her waist in the process. "I'll wait for you to get in touch."

She turned her back on both men and walked to the door.

The doorman nodded a polite goodnight to her as she left the club. She returned it but barely, knowing that both men were following her. In the dark, stuffy alley, she turned in the direction of the Main Canal, a less circuitous route out of the Docks. The two men were at her side within three steps like a couple of watchdogs.

"Very inconspicuous," she mumbled under her breath.

When a shadow detached itself from a nearby wall and hurried in the opposite direction, Kira decided maybe conspicuous wasn't always a bad thing. In a low tone she hoped wouldn't carry in the echoing quiet of the streets, she said to Raf, "I thought you had business."

He glanced over his shoulder, then faced straight ahead again. "Just keep going toward the Grand Bridge."

David didn't look behind them, but she felt him tense. "Are you armed?" he asked the pilot.

"Yes. You?"

"Yes."

"Kira?" Raf whispered.

"Small blaster, but only strong enough to stun." She ignored the sideways, appraising glance David shot her. They were walking at a steady, unhurried pace, the Main Canal within sight through the narrow walkway. From the canal, they had only to walk to their left for another two hundred meters to reach the bridge out of the Docks.

Every nerve ending screamed at Kira to run and run fast, but she'd gotten used to this tension and uncertainty over the last five years. She knew how to control her anxiety. She also knew, without looking, that they were being followed none too discreetly. The streets ahead of them were cleared or clearing quickly—in anticipation.

"How'd you get here?" Raf asked her, glancing over his shoulder again. When he turned forward, he placed one hand on her elbow. The move put his hand that much closer to his weapon.

"Public transport rail."

From the corner of her eye, she saw Raf grin. "Didn't trust bringing your own transport close to the Docks?"

"No." She couldn't help her slight smile.

"I've got a car not too far from the bridge," David murmured.

Raf nodded and steered Kira out onto the walkway that bordered the Main Canal. Boats sat moored to thick wooden pilings along the edge of the canal. A few small gondolas drifted soundlessly by on the black water. The fresher air along the canal was thick with the scent of sea, kelp and fish. Lamplight colored the walk a hazy orange-pink that might have been romantic if not for the utter silence filling the light and shadows. The only sounds Kira heard were those of her boot heels clicking along the flagstones and the pounding of blood in her ears.

They were within sight of the Grand Bridge, only a short sprint to its edge, when a rough growl rose behind them. "You may as well stop now, Raf."

Raf stilled but nodded for Kira and David to continue. She wanted to protest, but David took her other elbow and began walking her to the bridge.

"Nope," the growling voice behind them said. "The others stay, too."

"This is between you and me, Gavuq," Raf said, his voice low.

Kira and David stopped and turned slowly around. The owner of the growling voice was impossibly thin and tall. He stood well over seven feet, but he looked to be made of no more than bone. He wore a dark cloak over a billowing maroon robe of embroidered silk. His face was as pale as Narava's two moons. His eyes glowed fluorescent yellow in the dim light. The hood of the cloak covered the top of his head, but Kira knew that beneath it he was bald.

"I told you once before, Gavuq," Raf said in an even, confident voice, "I don't traffic your kind. There was no deal broken. You got your money back. So it's time you take your dogs off my tail."

"You deceived us," Gavuq hissed.

"Listen, you son of a bitch, I was the one misled. You knew from the start I wouldn't deal with your kind. Not after what happened on the *Venture*."

"And yet you returned to the Docks to seek me out," Gavuq said with a mocking bow of his skeletal head. He spread his arms, palms upraised.

"To tell you to back the fuck off," Raf said. "I won't carry Leeches on my ship, no matter the money and no matter the threat. Find someone else, Gavuq. But don't fuck with me anymore."

Kira felt the shifting of cool autumn air before she saw shadows roll up from the steps leading down to the water of the canal. There were at least ten of them, all tall and skeletal. And deadly.

She flexed her right hand and a small stunner dropped into her palm from the holster strapped to her forearm. It wouldn't kill the Leeches, it might not even stun them for long, but it would sure as hell slow them down. Raf already had his weapon in hand and was backing toward David and Kira. They moved back to back, watching the Leeches surround them.

CHAPTER THREE

My parents are worried about me. I've been dating Eian for three months now, and I'm in love. But my dad refuses to accept him. And worse, mom is urging me to break off the relationship. She's always been so easygoing about the men I date. They both say they're just trying to protect me, but protect me from what? Eian is ambitious and strong, confident and in control all the time. He'll be a commander soon. He makes me feel safe. Why wouldn't my parents want that for me?

—From the journal of Kira Farseaker

"WHAT NOW?" David asked without taking his eyes off the menacing shadows forming a circle around them.

"Make a hole," Raf said. "Get over the bridge. We can make a run for it from there."

Kira tensed, waiting for the first attack. It came from her left.

The sound of a blaster pierced the silence and left the scent of scorched molecules in the air. As the single Leech hit by the shot fell to the flags, the rest of the group swarmed in on Kira, Raf and David. Kira fired, not really aiming, just working to keep the stretched limbs and fingers away from her. Her small blaster did little more that punch the Leeches backward a step or two, disorienting them for several seconds, but never long enough to create an escape hole.

The scent of fried skin and the hiss and growl of the Leeches surrounded her. A long white fingertip made its way past the blaster fire to touch Kira's bare thigh. The patch of skin went numb and Kira screeched, a sound at once appalled, startled and angry. She shot the finger from her skin in the same instant, surprised to see it shatter under the close-range power of her little weapon. Before she had time to consider that reaction, however, a second hand moved too close, and she fired with blind fury.

Then a hole opened up. She didn't wait to see who followed; she broke through and ran to the bridge. The numb patch on her thigh slowed her, making it more difficult to move that muscle. But determination and fear pushed her forward. She hit the stone bridge at a full run. Behind her, she heard the continued sounds of blaster fire and the low grunts and occasional high-pitched squeals of the injured Leeches.

On the opposite side of the bridge she slowed and turned, unsure where to go next. David and Raf were right behind her, still firing over their shoulders at the following shadows.

"This way," David yelled, and they ran toward a low, grassy hill.

David's vehicle was a small, purple two-door sportster that looked as smooth as it was fast. Kira would have laughed at his fortuitous choice of cars if she'd had enough air in her lungs. The Leeches would never catch them in that thing.

The doors flew open at David's shouted voice command. He stood at the passenger door, motioning her inside. Then a charge of blaster fire whizzed past her head and hit David square in the shoulder. He spun once and landed face-first on the soft shoulder of the road.

"Shit!" Kira dove for the ground, rolling David as another blaster shot sliced overhead. "David?" She shook him. He groaned, and his eyes fluttered open. "Damn it to hell. Don't die on me, Officer," she ordered.

"Never, pretty eyes," he murmured.

The compliment stilled her for a breath. Then she moved, dragging him to the open passenger door. Raf knelt at the side of the car, continuing to fire in the direction of the rogue blaster shots.

"I thought Leeches never used weapons," she shouted, trying to get David into the back of the sportster. He was just conscious enough to get most of the way into the car with her help. But when his upper body lurched onto the seat he passed out, leaving Kira to manhandle his legs into the rear. She pushed the seat back, then crawled in, sliding behind the wheel.

"Get in!" she shouted at Raf even as she started the engine. She'd apologize to David later for using an override command code on his car. It was an emergency precaution, bought at a substantial price, in case a quick escape was ever necessary. The only drawback was that it ended up frying the vehicle's circuits.

The engine roared to life. Raf dove in, still firing out the open door, only closing it when the car screeched forward.

"Where the hell was that blaster fire coming from?" Kira demanded as she punched the sportster into high gear down the curving highway.

"Damn me if I know! Maybe Gavuq wasn't taking a chance on me getting away."

Kira spared him a withering glance, then focused on the road ahead, working to keep from killing them at the speed she was driving. "We're going to talk about this later."

"Later. Right now, we need to hide. I don't think they'll shake off easily. And your friend in the back needs help."

Kira nodded, fishtailing around a corner and heading for familiar ground.

"Hey, where the hell are you going?" Raf demanded. "The city's in the opposite direction. What kind of help are we gonna find in the suburbs?"

She smiled humorlessly. "My kind of help. Is our deal still on, Tygran?"

"Absolutely. Only the date's moved up. I need to be off planet within the next couple of days. Before the Leeches track down my ship."

"Shit," she spat, then whipped around another corner. *"Xep!"* she called out telepathically, hoping she was close enough to reach the Shifter. She'd deal with the headache this effort would cause later.

"Kira?"

The mind voice wasn't Xep's, but it was familiar nonetheless. *"Daq, I'm coming in fast and on the run. We're on*

Marshal Avenue in a purple sportster. I've got Raf Tygran with me and another man who's been wounded."

"Jo is opening the Creek entrance for you now."

"Thanks, Daq. Tell Sam to be ready."

She shot around a horseshoe bend and up a low rise. When she crested the small hill, the road evened out and followed a thin, swift-moving creek toward a larger, bare hill. To the left of the road, opposite the creek, a number of mansions commanded a view of the Dreic Sea, unmarred by the sight of the Docks farther down the coast.

"Brace yourself," Kira warned as she drove straight for the bare hill where the road dead-ended.

"What the—?"

Raf didn't have time to say more as Kira drove into the hard earth…and through it into a narrow cavern.

"Hologram," she told him, bringing the vehicle to a stop. As she disengaged the engine, the dash fizzled and hissed before shorting out. Sighing, Kira lifted the door manually and rolled out.

They were surrounded immediately by a handful of humans and Shifters. "Sam." Kira nodded to the medic, a short, well-muscled man in his late fifties. "Take care of him, please. But keep him unconscious until I decide what to do with him."

"What about you?" Sam frowned down at her leg.

For the first time since the Leech had touched her, Kira looked at her numb thigh. A circle of skin was black and sunken, as if some of the muscle beneath had been removed. She didn't feel anything, but the sight of the wound made her stomach roll.

"It's nothing." She brushed away Sam's attempt to

examine the injury more closely. "I'll get it taken care of in a little while. Right now, the man in the car needs your attention more than I do. He was hit in the shoulder with a blaster shot."

Sam nodded reluctantly, knowing she was right about which wound was more life-threatening. He moved to the car where two other men gently lifted David out of the backseat and onto a gurney. David stirred under the handling and opened his eyes. They were bright and wild-looking. And he was staring right at one of the Shifters helping Sam.

The medic administered a fast-acting anesthetic knock-out, putting David under again before they settled him on the gurney. Kira could only hope he wouldn't remember this later. She watched until they wheeled David out of sight down one of the corridors branching away from the cavern. Fiddling with the ends of her jacket, worry momentarily made her forget there were others around.

A gentle, cautious touch on her shoulder brought her back to her surroundings. She met Daq's multifaceted purple-blue gaze and smiled faintly. *"Thanks. Where's Jo?"*

"Command. Don't worry, Kira. Sam will see to the man. He will recover."

"I know." Kira's brow furrowed. *"But he's one of Ennoren's, Daq."*

The Shifter dropped its hand. After a silent minute, Daq said, *"It's no matter, Kira. He was wounded. You did the right thing."*

"But what am I going to do with him now?"

"You will think of something." Daq conveyed a confident "feel" that wasn't like a tone of voice, more a touch of

emotion. It was the direct conveyance of abstract thought and feeling that human telepaths couldn't manage.

"I'm glad someone here is confident in my abilities," Kira murmured aloud. Then she remembered who she'd called to first. *"Where's Xep?"*

Daq hesitated, glancing at Raf. The pilot lounged against the side of the now useless sportster, chatting easily with a couple of Kira's people. Breeanne was at the front of the group, legs braced, distrust etched in her large, pretty face and deep in her gray eyes. Kira could tell by the woman's stance that she was grilling Raf on the events of the evening. When she pointed at Kira's leg, Kira knew she was demanding an explanation.

She almost felt sorry for Raf, having to face Breeanne when her ire was up. Until she saw the wicked, flirty glint in his blue eyes. Then she felt sorry for Breeanne.

"Raf?" Kira called telepathically, a test that was hard to hide from when taken off guard. Most telepaths, whether they realized they were or not, had trouble hiding all signs of reaction when a voice dropped into their heads unexpectedly. Raf didn't even twitch. He kept smiling up at Breeanne, who was taller than him, while he leaned against the car and continued answering her battery of questions.

"He's not telepathic," Kira told Daq.

Daq still hesitated. Taking Kira's arm, the Shifter steered her toward a tunnel next to the one where Sam had taken David for treatment. Before she could be led away entirely, however, Kira called to Breeanne. "Make sure the pilot is given a room. And if it makes you feel better, Bree, keep a guard on him. You could even do it yourself."

She grinned at Bree's scowl, while Raf bellowed out a

laugh that echoed in the cavern. He winked at Kira, and she smiled back before allowing Daq to move her down the hall.

At the end of a short walk, the corridor branched out in three directions. Daq indicated they continue down the right tunnel, toward the area the Shifters who lived in the complex called home. They didn't go far before Daq stopped and opened a brass-inlaid door. The room beyond was bare but for a pile of pillows in one corner, a stack of paper books in another and a low table in the center of the room with a large flower and plant arrangement growing out of the wooden tabletop.

"Why are we in Xep's room?" Kira looked up at the Shifter who still seemed nervous, though she couldn't have explained why she got that impression. The Shifters didn't reveal their frame of mind with anything as easy to read as a facial expression.

"Your blaster." Daq reached out a slim, golden-skinned hand, and Kira placed the small weapon on the Shifter's palm. Daq set the blaster on the floor. An instant later, Xep stood where the weapon had been.

Kira's eyes widened and her mouth dropped. Upset, she switched to speaking aloud. "Xep? Shit."

"I am sorry, Kira." Xep said, shifting its face into a human form so she would see the contrite expression. *"But I didn't want you going into the Docks alone at night."*

"Damn it, what if something had happened?"

"Something did happen," Xep reminded her.

"I meant, what if David had had a detector on him? What if there were scans on the door at the club?"

"None of that happened. Besides, I was not in organic

form. And I'm free to come and go as I see fit, Kira. I take my chances, as do you."

Her shoulders dropped. It was hard to be angry when Xep was right. "Sorry," she mumbled. "But you should have told me you were with me." She switched back to mind speech, though her head was already beginning to ache. *"What if I'd had to abandon the blaster for some reason?"*

Xep nodded. *"That part was foolish. I didn't think you'd allow my company, though."*

A thought suddenly hit her. *"You fired through the Leech's finger, didn't you?"*

She knew her palm blaster didn't have the power to cut through bone and muscle, even at close range. She'd been too busy at the time to really consider it.

"I did. I don't like Leeches."

Kira stared into the whirling blue and purple of Xep's eyes for a minute. Then nodded. *"I don't like them, either."*

She didn't mention what was left unsaid between them, that Shifters were naturally so non-violent that humans had come close to wiping them out. Nor did she mention that, until that instant, Xep had never personally hurt another creature.

Evolution in progress, she thought sadly to herself. The ability to injure wasn't the only newly evolved trait in the Shifters—it was just the one she most regretted.

CHAPTER FOUR

I saw a Shifter today! At least, I think I did. I was walking Dabber, our peuchow, not far from the house and caught a flash of gold in the trees. When I looked, I swear I saw this thin golden shape with whirling blue and green eyes. Then I blinked and it was gone, just a bunch of trees remained. It was terrifying! Those things could be anywhere. SCR has proven they're dangerous and eat meat. Eian says he's seen the bodies of those attacked by Shifters.

Dabber and I ran the rest of the way home.

—From the journal of Kira Farseaker

DAVID ROLLED onto his side with a groan then immediately wished he hadn't. The pain was a slow burn that started in his shoulder and spread over his entire body.

"Hold still a minute," a quiet, familiar voice ordered.

He felt a sharp prick in his uninjured arm, and within seconds the ache eased. Slowly, he opened his eyes. The golden brown eyes he looked into were bright with concern. He smiled despite his grogginess.

"Kira," he greeted, pleased when the concern turned to relief. She'd shed the trendy and expensive red mini-dress, which he found a little disappointing, and replaced it with a simple pair of brown leggings, a fitted brown high-collar tunic and a short mustard-colored vest. The leggings helped make up for the loss of the mini-dress.

His gaze swept back to her face. He had an almost overwhelming urge to reach up and run a hand through her amber hair where it fell over the collar of her vest. The shade was nearly an exact match for the color of her eyes, but there were a few streaks of red in her hair. And he wanted to trace those lines of russet. Without thinking, he tried to stretch his hand toward her and was painfully reminded of his injury.

"Lie still," she ordered, settling him onto his back and tucking the blanket around his chest without looking directly at him.

The brush of her hands against the bare skin of his chest and shoulders warmed him from the gut out. After a moment, she glanced up and met his gaze. "How do you feel?"

"Like shit. How 'bout you?"

She smiled. "I'm not the one that got hit with a blaster shot."

"No, but I saw the Leech wound on your leg before I passed out."

"Oh. It's fine. Sam grafted new skin and muscle in its place, so I'm good as new."

David frowned. "Sam? The medic?"

"He said you came to briefly."

"Then he knocked me out again. Where are we?"

She flinched and stood, pacing away from the bed to the door and back, absently tugging at the edges of her vest. The movement put David on alert, wary of what her nervous gesture meant. After several laps of the room, she stopped beside his bed and looked down at him, her expression too serious for his liking.

"I'm sorry about this. But I'm in a tricky situation at the moment. And you work for Ennoren."

"Not Ennoren again," he muttered, resenting his association with the man once more. "What's your ex-husband got to do with this?"

"It's a long story." She let out a loud breath, her gaze pleading with him to understand. "I…I'm involved in something… And I can't trust you because you're with the Guard, but more importantly, because you work for Eain. He'll go to great lengths to put me under his control again, or to break me, whichever comes first. And I can't allow that. I've got too much at stake right now."

"It's the Shifters, isn't it?" He hardened his voice and his emotions. He didn't like the direction this conversation had taken. He hadn't wanted to believe his eyes, to believe the accusations Ennoren had tossed at her. But the evidence was all around him. "I've seen them here. Are you hiding them? Trying to protect them from the law?"

She straightened, her pleading look vanishing behind an emotionless stare. "You'll have to remain here for the next week. You'll be released—"

"Released?" he interrupted. "I'm a prisoner?" He very

nearly sat up in bed. Only the sharp stab of pain in his shoulder and a rush of dizziness forced him back against the pillow.

"You'll be released," she continued as if he hadn't spoken, "when there's no longer a chance that you can lead Ennoren to us. I've no other choice. Your needs will be taken care of. One more session with Sam, and your wound will be almost completely healed."

Not even a trace of the emotions he'd seen just moments ago leaked into her voice. That coldness made him angrier than being kept a prisoner. "Damn it, Kira! After the Docks, I'd bloody well think you'd give me more consideration than that."

"Why?" she asked evenly.

When he could only stare at her in shock at the simple question, she continued. "If I were a better leader, David, I'd have left you behind. I compromised both my people and my mission by bringing you here."

Her words were like ice dropping onto his stomach. Burning even as they froze. This wasn't the way things were supposed to happen. She wasn't really supposed to be a terrorist. "Ennoren was right about you," he whispered, anger overwhelming his good sense. "The Commander said a viper lived beneath your skin. I didn't believe him. Now I see I misjudged you."

Her jaw flexed as she clenched her teeth. Her gaze moved to the white wall behind him.

"I'll have Sam come in to tend your injury now." She turned and left the room without looking at him.

But that hadn't prevented him from seeing the single tear slip down her cheek.

David cursed at the ceiling, long and graphically. Torn between guilt, fury and impotence, he was still grumbling when the door slid open and the medic, Sam, walked in. David had only vague memories of the man, fuzzy and distorted by pain and knockouts. But Sam wasn't nearly as tall as David had first thought. He was short, really. His thick gray hair was tied in a low tail. His clean-shaven, angular face and large hands were deep reddish-brown, and though both were lined with age, the medic moved with the ease and grace of a much younger man.

He settled onto the edge of the bed and examined David's wound, first with his hands, then with a small med-scan. David watched, resenting the older man for no good reason but that he was one of Kira's people. Another terrorist. Sam ignored the angry gaze, going about his job with cool efficiency.

When he'd finished scanning David's injured shoulder, he took an epidermal skimmer from the table beside the narrow bed and ran it rhythmically over the wound. Since Kira had already given him another shot of painkiller, David didn't feel anything but a slight tingle as the medic slowly repaired the damaged tissue around his shoulder.

"You'll have some trouble with this shoulder for a few months, a bit of stiffness, until the muscles fully recover," Sam told him, "but it'll heal well with only a little scarring."

"I don't get a skin graft?" David asked acidly.

Sam paused, but his detached expression never changed. "I don't like you enough to give you a full skin graft. They cost too much, and you're not worth it."

The medic resumed his work, leaving David glowering.

When Sam finished with the skimmer, he set his equipment on the table next to the bed and met David's gaze. David returned the stare without flinching. He'd be damned if he'd be intimidated by the older man. He'd faced worse in the last twelve years.

"She didn't deserve that, you know?" Sam said in a hushed voice. "She's under enough pressure as it is. She's doing the best she can."

"For herself, maybe," David shot back.

"For the people around her. For the people who depend on her for their very lives. She's taken on a great deal of responsibility in the last four years. More than she should have. More than anyone should have to."

"If you're trying for my sympathy, you're wasting your breath. She's a terrorist, harboring Shifters, breaking the law. Besides, I'm the one who's the prisoner here."

"She has to keep you here. It won't be for long." Sam stood and turned toward the door. "And if it were me, I would have chucked you out onto an abandoned street with a memory wipe. But that's just me."

David watched the door close behind the medic, not sure whether to shout or curse or spit. He settled on another round of cursing. He cursed the medic, the Shifters, the room he was confined to. He cursed Ennoren and Senator Rodriguez for putting him in this position. He cursed the Leeches for attacking them, the other man that had been with Kira for bringing the Leeches down on them, the unknown bastard who'd shot him. And most fervently, he cursed himself and his weakness for the golden brown eyes of a terrorist.

KIRA RUBBED her cheek when she felt a hand on her arm, but she didn't turn around. "How is he?"

"Well enough," Sam said. "How are you?"

"Fine."

"I've known you for too many years for you to lie to me that badly."

She felt a small smile tug at her mouth, but it lost its battle to form. She sighed and faced the old medic. "It's just… He doesn't deserve this. To be held against his will like this. Especially after…"

"Kira, you're doing what you have to do."

"I know, it's just…" She let the sentence trail off. She didn't know how to put the feeling into words that Sam would understand, the feeling that she was betraying David in some way.

"Have you ever stopped to consider why he was at the Docks last night? Xep told me how you two met. Why would he turn up, just like that, seemingly by accident in an area where Guards don't go?"

"I know. I know. Of course I've thought of it, and I'm sure I've reached the same conclusion you have. Ennoren sent him to spy on me, maybe to seduce me for information because I showed an interest in him at the blockade. And even if all that weren't true, David is still a Guard, and he's seen the Shifters. According to government and police policy, he has to report their location to the exterminators now." She took a deep, shaky breath, then spread her arms helplessly. "But knowing all that doesn't change my guilt."

The older man rested a hand on her shoulder, considering her for a quiet moment. He nodded, pursing his lips, and moved past her down the corridor. "You've always felt responsible for the feelings and circumstances of those around you," he said as he walked away. "When do you start taking time for your own feelings?"

She watched him disappear around a bend in the corridor. Then quietly, to the empty hall, she murmured, "When I have time. And right now, I don't have the time."

A familiar feeling began to twist in her gut, overwhelming and cancerous. Helplessness, impatience, knowing that she had too much to do and all of it a race against time, against Ennoren. And above all of that was guilt. Guilt that she couldn't be everything, do everything for everyone.

She stared at the door leading into David's small medroom. She had other things to do, other worries, other responsibilities. But at that moment, all she really wanted to do was go back into that room and ask his forgiveness, beg his understanding and patience. The good man that watched her from those coffee-colored eyes had to understand why she was doing all this. She just needed to explain. He wasn't Ennoren.

But he was a Guard. A Guard under Ennoren's command. And he was very angry with her at the moment.

A quiet blip sounded at her waist. She lifted her pocketcomm from her vest pocket and answered the request. "Kira here."

"Kira." Vettine's voice sounded out of the credit card-sized internal communicator. "Jo needs you in Command. And that pilot says he has to talk to you. You also promised Xep a brief meeting this morning."

Kira took a deep breath before answering. It seemed her

choices had once again been made for her. "Tell Jo I'll be up in five. Kira out." She slipped the pocket-comm back into her vest and took one last, longing look at the door. Then she turned up the hall and headed toward the command center of the complex.

CHAPTER FIVE

The debate over the Shifter issue is getting more violent. The protesters, though a minority, have increased their efforts lately. Eian says they're a small group of radicals, nothing to worry about. Most of the planet still supports the exterminations. My mom and dad disagree. But they're not on the front line like Eian. How can they know what's really going on?

I'm worried about Eian, though. He's at most of those protests and there's been violence.

—From the journal of Kira Farseaker

SOMEWHERE IN THE midst of his damning the universe and everything in it, David fell back to sleep. When he woke, the painkillers had worn off. The ache wasn't so bad this time. He tried moving his shoulder, cautious against the possibility of more pain, and studied with grudging respect the masterfully tended wound. Only a faint scar remained. Better treatment than he'd expected from the medic.

After a few minutes, when the ache didn't get any worse, he hazarded more movement and sat up in bed. He was hungry. There were no windows in the room so he couldn't judge what time it was, but his stomach told him it was probably well into the afternoon. He glanced around the small room and spotted his clothes laid neatly over a fold-out metal chair. With a grimace, he swung his feet to the side of the bed and stood. A rush of dizziness sat him back on the bed with a bounce.

"Shit." As the dizziness passed and his vision cleared, he tried to stand again. This time he managed to keep his feet under him. He pulled on his black pants and turtleneck, gritting his teeth against the groan that threatened at the back of his throat. He had to sit down to catch his breath after getting dressed. He focused on the white wall across from him, trying to ignore the faint medicinal scent that permeated the room. Then, with a determined breath, he leaned over to put on his boots. The combination of knockout after-effects and hunger left him weaker than he liked. After finishing with his boot laces, he rested his forearms on his knees, letting his head droop. Being held by terrorists wasn't a good time to be weak. Food. He needed food.

He took a deep breath and stood. When dizziness didn't drop him back onto the chair, he walked to the door. To his surprise, it wasn't locked. In the corridor beyond, where he'd expected a guard, he was met with only quiet air and steel-plated walls. Frowning, David stepped out into the hall and looked down the identical lengths of steel tubing curving off into either direction. He turned to his left.

As he walked, he patted the pockets of his pants, then cursed that he hadn't thought to check his jacket for his cigarettes. With a sigh, he continued down the corridor. The more he walked, the more balanced he felt, less drugged and helpless. His stomach continued to grumble, but the weakness was receding, leaving his mind clearer. He didn't like the way drugs made him feel, even when they were pain relievers. The fogginess and slowed reflexes left him too vulnerable. He detested being vulnerable.

Turning down another unmarked hall, he followed a faint hint of voices, or maybe the buzz of machinery. The lights overhead flickered on as he passed, then off behind him, leaving the way he'd come in shadows. He stopped and glanced over his shoulder. Would he be able to find his way back?

Hell with it. If they wanted him locked in that particular room, they'd take him back to it.

Just as he was turning to continue toward the distant noise, he thought he saw a movement behind him in the darkened hall. The overhead lighting didn't come on. He rubbed the back of his neck. If someone were there, their movement would have turned on the lights. He started walking again, but the nagging feeling that someone was behind him didn't stop until he stepped out of the corridor and into what was undoubtedly the command center of the complex.

One wall was covered with screens displaying areas of the complex, what looked to be rooms in a richly decorated house, the front door of a mansion and several outside views —none of which he recognized. A number of the screens also displayed local and interplanetary news broadcasts. One screen, he noticed with something close to amazement, even monitored the Guards' private communications channel.

The screens showing views inside the complex, however, provided the answer to his suspicion that he was being followed. The vids would have recorded his movement, and someone in this room must have watched him pass through the halls. He allowed a grudging amount of respect for that alertness. No good terrorist should leave a prisoner unmonitored.

The center of the large, well-lit room was taken up by a multi-base port computer system. Three people sat around the square, monitoring the screens before them and voicing in comments, commands and requests. Beyond them, five doors left the area.

To his right, what he guessed to be a communications board took up half the wall. The other half was covered by a huge tapestry depicting an early scene of the first humans on Narava. A man with long, straight black hair, sharp but handsome features, deep red-brown skin and golden brown eyes played a central role in the action of the intricately woven wall hanging. Beside the man stood a woman in flight gear with waist-length red hair and dark brown eyes that seemed to flicker with life from within the two-dimensional picture.

The tapestry held him fascinated. It seemed so out of place amidst all the surrounding technology, and yet it seemed the very heart of the room. David studied the man in the center of the tapestry, staring at his golden brown eyes as if they held some knowledge, some answers. When the portrait didn't give up any secrets, he turned his attention back to the room, hunting for one face in particular.

She stood near the wall of view screens, talking in hushed tones with the man that had run from the Docks with them. David finally recognized him. He hadn't remembered him before this moment, but now he recalled his image from the Guards' mainframe wanted list. Raf Tygran, pilot, smuggler, hustler and thief. And, David thought with a faint snarl, womanizer.

A slow, building anger churned in the center of his gut, tensing his muscles. He couldn't have explained the anger. Of the many reasons he had to be pissed at that moment, he couldn't have named which was the real cause. And he didn't care. He warmed himself with the rage, letting it strengthen his concentration, focus his confused emotions. He watched their discussion, watched the way Kira pushed her amber hair behind her ears, the way her forehead crinkled when she frowned, the concentration in her golden brown eyes.

He'd attracted attention when he'd entered the room. Other people glanced at him with nervous or hesitant expressions, but no one approached and asked his business. That was good. It gave him time to slow his pulse and control his emotions before approaching Kira and Raf. He needed his anger to remind him that he was a prisoner and she was a terrorist, but he couldn't afford to let the emotion get the best of him. Control. He had to remain focused.

He took in his surroundings one last time, then walked toward Kira. She hadn't noticed him yet. Her focus was on the pirate. As he watched, her frown turned up to a smile, then a great booming laugh echoed in the cavernous room. The sound vibrated through him like a single clear note through a tuning fork. He flicked a look to Tygran to see him grinning at her like a cat. David jammed his fists into his pockets to keep from using them on the pirate. The irrational desire to smash Tygran's pretty face for making Kira laugh disturbed him. Disturbed him as much as her laughter had disturbed his focus.

Why should it bother him that Tygran made her laugh?

He forced his misgivings aside, not willing to examine his own motivations too closely. He would simply dislike Tygran on principle. And if the need arose to pound on the man a little, well, he wasn't one to argue with necessity.

Because he was watching, David saw Kira stiffen when she noticed him. Her face closed up, cutting off the brilliant laughter that had been there a moment before and replacing it with wariness. Tygran noticed the change too and took a step closer to her when David stopped next to them. The protective gesture irritated David almost as much as Tygran's ability to make Kira smile. He clenched his fists and kept them wedged in his pockets. *Control, Cario. Focus. You have things you need to do, answers you need to find. No time to let a pair of pretty eyes bother you.*

He didn't acknowledge the pilot, but put the full force of his fluctuating anger into his gaze as he stared at Kira. She was keeping him prisoner against his will. She was a terrorist. She was Ennoren's ex-wife, and therefore off limits. She represented all the things in his past that had brought him to this point.

And damn it all to hell if she wasn't making it easy for him to forget why all of that was a bad thing. Just looking into those wide, golden brown eyes shook his control, blurred his focus, made him question his resolve. He had a job to do. Kira was part of that job, nothing more. She was the enemy, everything that Ennoren said she was.

So why the hell did he want so badly to kiss her?

"Kira," he growled after a tense and silent moment. He let his anger burn in his voice, hoping it would hide his desire, needing it to hide his weakness.

She flinched. Part of David triumphed in that small victory. Another part regretted it.

She nodded at Tygran. "I'll talk with you later, Raf."

David sensed the smuggler stiffening at the dismissal, but he didn't turn. He kept his gaze on Kira's face, watching every twitch, every emotion sliding through her eyes. He was desperate to hold on to his anger now. Watching that beautiful, expressive face drained away his rage. He wasn't sure he wanted to be in her presence without the anger as a defense.

"I've got to contact my co-pilot," Raf said. "I'll meet you later, Kira?"

"Yes."

Then David and Kira were alone. She focused on a spot just past his ear. "How's your shoulder?"

"Fine. Sam left less scarring than he threatened to."

She quirked a brow at that and her lips crooked up just a bit. "He can't seem to help being good at his job." Affection for the medic leaked out in her voice. "You must need food." She snapped back to business. "I didn't think you'd be up and about just yet. I'll have Grainne show you to the dining hall."

"Why not you?"

"I have work to do."

"Buildings to blow up, people to kill."

His comment made her eyes flare wide, and she finally met his gaze. "What the hell does that mean?"

"Isn't that what terrorists do? You are a terrorist, aren't you, Kira?"

"I most certainly am not!" The startled looks her explosion drew from the others in the room made her drop her voice to a harsh whisper. "I don't have time to trade insults and accusations with you. Now…"

"Yes, now. You and I are going to talk. Now. Make time."

"You son of a bitch. Who the hell do you think you are?"

"Your prisoner."

She stepped back as if she'd been slapped. "I told you that couldn't be helped. I'm sorry. I know you don't believe that, but I am." She took a steadying breath. "We both know you'd have to report this compound to Ennoren. You've seen the Shifters, and it's your duty. I can't let you do that."

"Why didn't you just wipe my mind and dump me on the road like Sam suggested?"

"Because I don't believe in mind wipes. Too many side effects, and too dangerous to you. Your entire memory could get erased by accident."

The explanation confirmed something about her that he'd been afraid to believe after their earlier conversation. His anger wavered, then began to wane. Walking into the command center, he'd wanted, needed to think the worst of her. Now she was confirming his very first impression. He flashed on the image of her in ripped jeans and a flannel shirt, facing him from behind the steering wheel of her van, on the memory of that familiar something in her eyes that had drawn him even more than her beauty. And he acknowledged something about her that Ennoren hadn't admitted. She wasn't ruthless or heartless. She had honor.

But that knowledge also blurred the lines of his mission

further. He remained silent for a long time, holding her gaze. Then he asked, "Do you have any cigarettes?"

His question seemed to surprise her. She blinked, then smiled. David's gut tightened and a rush of heat pulsed through his veins in response.

"I don't smoke," she said, "but I can get you some. I'm afraid you'll have to confine your smoking to certain areas of the complex, though. It's not good for the Shifters to be exposed to too much cigarette smoke."

"Why not?" He frowned. It wasn't too healthy for humans to be exposed to it, either, but he suspected she wasn't talking about lung cancer and heart attacks.

She studied him then, assessing what she saw. For the first time in years, he had to work not to fidget under that kind of scrutiny.

"You don't know much about Shifters, do you?"

He shrugged. "As much as most people know." He jammed his hands farther into his pockets, uncomfortable with having shown her his ignorance.

"That's not much," she said with a sad shake of her head. "Shifters feed directly from nutrients in the air. Their cells take up needed molecules from the surrounding environment, so they can feed even when they aren't in their natural form. That means that they can take up poisonous molecules from the air too, like tar."

She fell silent, pursing her lips, then turned to the computer block at the center of the room. "Grainne."

She caught the attention of a thin-faced, red-haired girl who was chewing the edge of a mouse-stylus. "I'm going to show our…guest," she nodded to David, "around and get him some food. Beep me when Pat gets back, and let Jo know that

Raf's gonna need help with some of our supplies. Oh, and have James meet me in the canteen with a pack of cigarettes."

At the woman's nod, Kira turned back to him. She tilted her head toward a nearby door and indicated with a hand that they should go. He walked beside her in silence through a series of corridors. The anger that had followed him from his med-room was vanishing. He was no less her prisoner now than he had been twenty minutes ago, but that fact bothered him less and less. Oh, he still didn't like having his free will inhibited—hated it, in fact. But he was where he needed to be, sooner than he thought to get here. He glanced down at the woman beside him, caught her brushing an amber lock of hair behind her ear, and knew that the sooner he got this mission over with, the better.

He glanced around as she led him through an open doorway into a large canteen. The long, rectangular metal tables that filled most of the room were empty.

"You missed the midday meal rush and you're too early for the evening meal," Kira told him with a grin. "Good timing." She led him to a series of auto-cookers lining the far wall. "Coffee?" When he nodded, she ordered two cups. "What would you like to eat?"

"Doesn't matter."

She thought a moment, then ordered a bowl of mushroom soup and a loaf of warmed bread. "Tastes good after you've been under knockouts."

"My Irish granny used to make mushroom soup by hand for me when I was a kid," he told her. "Swore by its rejuvenating properties."

She grinned again. "Mine, too."

"My Italian granny swore by the healing effects of minestrone." No longer able to resist, he reached out and touched her jaw with his fingertips. His gaze dropped to her mouth when she licked her lips. "They argued about which was better for years."

"I'm not making you choose sides, am I?" Her voice was quiet.

"No." He traced her lower lip with his thumb. She sucked in a sharp breath, and his heart pounded in a rush of masculine triumph at that small, telling sound. "They took turns winning the argument. The last time I was sick, I had minestrone. It's Granny McGuire's turn to win."

"Oh," she whispered.

The sound of bleeping from the auto-cooker startled them both and shattered the moment. David dropped his hand and took a deep, slow breath.

Kira pulled the soup from the open door of the cooker and handed it to him without meeting his gaze. There was a slight pink tint to her cheeks that filled David with satisfaction as he took the plate of bread. He followed her to one of the long tables and sat, unable to look away from her for long. So many emotions and thoughts passed through her eyes.

He was in trouble. He'd been in dangerous situations before, but none this hazardous. And it wasn't just the threat of physical harm that scared him. After his years with the Guard, he was used to that possibility. No, this was a more personal threat, one that could do more damage than all the blasters on Narava. Confronted with the harm Kira could do to him, he would have preferred facing an army of Binnean warriors.

They sat in silence for a few moments while he sipped his soup and studied her. Then she pulled a small card-shaped device from her vest pocket and tapped a point on its surface. "Command code: Farseaker, K. Begin Tchyvonian's Symphony number eight. Level three."

The room filled with a light orchestral arrangement at a volume loud enough to cover the silence but quiet enough to make conversation easy.

She slid the card back into her vest. At his raised eyebrows, she winced. "I don't like total silence around food," she said. "I know it's silly, but I've never liked listening to other people, or myself for that matter, eat and drink."

He nodded, trying to stifle a grin. Her cheeks colored again, and she took a long drink of her coffee in an attempt to hide her embarrassment. His smile broke beyond his control. His anti-government terrorist leader didn't like to hear people chew. He chuckled and tore off a hunk of bread. She was…disarming.

Feeling generous because she'd just blushed twice in less than five minutes in front of him, he decided to change the subject. "Farseaker? Are you related to Nathaniel Farseaker?" he asked after swallowing a spoonful of soup.

Nathaniel was one of the first humans to settle Narava. He was a Navajo from Earth's North American continent and considered one of the greatest space explorers of his time. He was responsible for the discovery of more habitable planets than any other star hunter in history.

She smiled, familial pride shining in her eyes. "He was my paternal great-grandfather."

"That's him in the tapestry in your command center, isn't

it?" He thought he'd recognized the scene, knew he'd recognized the golden brown eyes. When she nodded, he said, "You have the same eyes, though your coloring is different."

"He married an Irish woman. The lighter coloring carried down through my dad's side of the family." She shrugged.

"Brigit Farseaker. I remember her from history lectures too. That's her in the tapestry also, then?" Brigit was one of the first pilots to fly beyond Earth's solar system. Her relationship with Nathaniel was reputed to be…turbulent at best.

Kira grinned. "That's her. I would have liked to have known her." She sighed. Then her expression turned serious again, and troubled. "David…I don't know where to start this conversation. I think you deserve an explanation of sorts, but… Well, the truth is, I can't trust the entire story to you. It would jeopardize too many lives if I were to tell you some things, but…" She stopped, puffing out a breath and running a hand through her hair in a distracted gesture.

"You could start by telling me why you're harboring a complex full of aliens."

"The Shifters aren't the aliens on this planet. We are. We stole their home from them, and then very nearly drove them to extinction. And if people like Ennoren and the planetary senators had their way, the Shifters would be extinct within the next few years. That can't be allowed."

All hesitancy left her voice and her demeanor. She spoke with a conviction that he couldn't deny she felt soul-deep. But he found it painful to hear and see a conviction that sincere. It was too damned familiar.

"Why?" he asked, his voice harsh with long-suppressed anger and pain. And guilt. "Why do you care so much what happens to them? They're little more than predatory mimics…"

"They are thinking, feeling, intelligent, cognizant creatures," she all but shouted. With an effort, she pulled in her temper. "Don't believe all the government's propaganda. Their so-called studies into the intellectual capabilities of the Shifters were a farce at best, designed to get public support for the exterminations. Shifters are not dangerous beasts lurking in corners, waiting to take over human bodies like parasites. They are not ravenous predators hunting humans. They lived here, evolved here for eons without the help of 'human hosts'."

"Then explain why the government would want to spend all this time and money on extermination? It doesn't make sense, Kira. If they're not a threat to humans, why bother?"

"Because there are those who know the truth and *do* consider them a threat. People with secrets to hide. People who think their power is challenged by the things a Shifter can do. Shifters evolve and adapt better than humans. They can be anywhere, at any time, and without a detector, humans would never know. Pretty scary concept if you don't know better. Add on supposed scientific 'evidence' that Shifters are vicious killers, and you think it was hard to convince the human population to support the exterminations? Rather than risk finding out the truth, most people are willing to turn the other way while this unknown is eliminated. It's an old story in human history." She dropped her angry gaze to her coffee mug. "We weren't ready," she murmured.

She spoke so quietly he almost didn't hear her over the building instrumental music. "Weren't ready for what?" He reached across the table and gripped one of her hands hard, urging her to look up. "What weren't we ready for?"

"For space travel, for meeting new species and cultures. It happened too fast. I sometimes wish Gerhaurst had never started his research into tachyons and warping drives. We weren't ready for the consequences of his breakthrough."

She made a sweeping gesture with her free hand. "We're too arrogant, we humans. We still assume we have rights over other creatures. Even after all the eons of evolution on Earth, all the experience and learning on Earth and in the galaxy, we assume we have the right to wipe out an entire species because they scare us. And because we can."

The sadness in her voice touched something in him. A deep part of himself that he'd suppressed for six years. He wanted to run away from that quiet sorrow and the memories it brought almost as much as he wanted to wipe it from her face. He moved his free hand to cup her cheek, caressing the silky skin with his thumb. "Is that what you're hoping to accomplish here, Kira? Are you hoping to change human arrogance?"

"All I want is to give the Shifters the chance they deserve. At life."

Beneath his palm, he felt her jaw muscles clench in an effort to maintain her control. But her eyes were dry and full of determination. David forgot about his meal, he forgot about his mission, he even forgot to be afraid of the consequences of being attracted to her. He leaned across the table, pulling her toward him with the hand on her cheek. When she didn't move away, he covered her lips with his.

He kissed her gently once. Then he kissed her again, deep and with a surprising hunger. He pushed his hand from her cheek into her hair and squeezed tight. She tasted of coffee and something sweet, unlike anything he'd tasted before. He ran his tongue over her lips, then urged them apart until she opened to him. A small moan sighed past her lips into his mouth, and David's entire body pulsed to a demanding need.

But before he could do more than grasp her shoulders to bring her closer, a bleeping sound exploded between them. Kira jerked away, gasping, her eyes wide and dark. David groaned and dropped back onto the bench, waiting for her to answer the pocket-comm. He ran a hand through his hair. But he couldn't tear his gaze from her lips.

After she took a few steadying breaths, she pulled the card from her vest pocket and answered the annoying summons. "Kira here." She focused on the table while she talked.

"Kira, Pat's back."

"Thanks, Jo. Did he manage everything?" There was a long pause. Kira frowned at the card in her hand. "Jo?"

"Honey, you'd better get down here. Pat has some news."

"On my way." Kira snapped off the comm and stood.

She stared down at him in a detached, appraising way that was all leader and none of the passionate woman he'd kissed moments before.

"You'd better come with me."

He looked past the stern expression into her eyes, and saw the fear. Standing, he followed her out of the canteen without another word.

CHAPTER SIX

EIAN ASKED ME TO MARRY HIM! WE'VE SET THE DATE FOR TWO months from now. It's going to be so perfect. I wish my parents were happier, though.

—From the journal of Kira Farseaker

COMMAND WAS silent when Kira walked in with David at her heels. All eyes turned to her, fearful and hopeful in a way that made Kira want to climb into a burrow and hide. Something was wrong, and they were worried. They also believed she'd be able to fix the problem.

She headed straight for Jo and the short, lanky man standing with her. Pat was in his mid-forties, but his black skin had yet to show any signs of aging. His bald head, trendy jeans and flannel shirt added to the air of youth about him. He was a genius at bargaining with the less-than-savory people Kira's group had to deal with. He was also a computer hacker of unequalled skill.

She greeted him with a brief nod. "What's the problem?"

Pat glanced at David, then back to her, his brow creasing. "Can we talk in your office?" he asked, his voice deeper than his thin frame suggested.

Kira studied Pat's expression for a moment before agreeing. "Jo, see to our guest, please. Make sure he gets some cigarettes and a place to smoke them. David." She turned to the Guard, ignoring the tiny shivers scurrying over her spine when she met his gaze. "We'll talk more later."

He inclined his head, his face expressionless, but his gaze was dark and full of heat.

Kira crossed the room to her office before she had time to worry about the heat. Pat followed her into the small, sparse room, and she closed the door. The room contained only two chairs and a small desk with a computer console and a communications board on it. She nodded toward a chair, offering Pat a seat, but he declined.

With a shrug, she settled herself on the corner of the desktop. "Okay, what's the problem?"

"First, the clearance code to leave planet is going to be harder to get than I thought."

"Why?" She half rose.

He raised a hand to settle her. "Not impossible. Just more difficult. Ennoren's upgraded the confirmation procedures and checks. I can still get it, but if you want it to work, it's gonna take a little more time."

"We don't have much time left, Pat. How long are we talking?"

"Couple of days at the most." She started to let out a relieved breath, but Pat shook his head. "That's not our only problem."

She frowned. "What else? The Guard hasn't found the new compound?"

"No. It's still secure. And they're almost up and running. They'll be able to take over once we've left. The problem is our new guest."

A sick tumble rolled through her gut. "Explain."

"He's been reported missing already."

"Already? Shit. I thought Ennoren would give him at least a few days before reporting it."

Pat grimaced. "Well, we just happened to have rescued the only member of the Guard that has never missed a day, an hour of duty in his entire career. I checked his record. David Cario is from a family of Guards, and he takes the position very seriously. Apparently, it wasn't even Ennoren that reported him absent. It was the duty sergeant. And, according to internal ears, the commander laid into the duty sergeant brutally. Threatened to send him up to the Nordien ice wastes. That part didn't make it to the news, however. Only the fact that a Guard has gone missing."

She took a deep breath, blew it out in a long, slow exhale that did little to untie the knots in her stomach. "Damn. Well, there's nothing for it now." She pushed her hair behind one ear. "We can't let him go yet. Not till we're gone and this complex has been shut down. He's seen too much. And before you say it—" she raised a warning eyebrow at his half-open mouth, "—I'm not wiping his memory. Period."

"We could kill him." Pat spoke without emotion.

"No," she said through clenched teeth, "we couldn't."

She forced her jaw to relax before continuing. Even the thought of killing David made her ill. But she couldn't very well tell Pat the real reason for her reticence. Instead, when she could trust her voice to sound calm, she told him her secondary but no less significant reason for keeping David alive. "I suspect Ennoren sent him to find me last night, to spy on me, maybe to gain my trust. I wouldn't be at all surprised if Ennoren knew David was with me last night."

Pat looked at his feet, one hand tugging at his full lower lip. "That would explain why he got so angry at the duty sergeant, I suppose. If he were trying to set you up, discover what and where you're hiding, he might have hoped that David would get pulled into your circle."

"And if David shows up dead now? He'll know we've found out he's a spy. It'll give Eain an excuse to descend on my house with a search warrant. Not his first choice, I imagine, since for all he knows, this place is clean. But a very viable alternative for him nonetheless. I'd guess the only reason he hasn't done it so far is that I haven't given him an excuse. Even Eain wouldn't want to offend some of my father's old associates. He'd need a reasonable explanation for the warrant. If David shows up dead, he'd have it. And we can't have him searching the estate yet."

"But after the newscast, won't Ennoren come asking questions anyway? Standard procedure. He wouldn't need a warrant for that. And I imagine there are at least one or two witnesses willing to say Cario was seen with you last night."

"From the Docks?" She raised a mocking brow. "I doubt it. But even if someone were able to connect us, that doesn't mean Ennoren would show up here personally. If he's sent David in as a spy, and there's a chance that David is still alive and maybe earning my trust right now, he won't want to hint to me that he knows I was with David last night. It would make me too suspicious. I might start to wonder how Eain knew about David and me at the Docks, how he knew to start asking questions there so soon. David's only been missing for one day. I'm sure there are a hundred other places they'd check first before the Docks, unless they already knew he'd been there."

She watched Pat take in her logic, nodding as he followed her reasoning. He might have argued the point with her, but he seemed prepared to hear her out. Fortunately. Because she really didn't want to explain that killing David would destroy something in her, something vital that she'd worked hard to hold on to during the last five years.

Settling her hands on the desk, she braced her weight, leaning back to better meet Pat's gaze. "If David shows up dead, Ennoren has nothing to lose by coming here. But until he knows David's fate, he can't risk blowing his cover. He can fend off the press with a made-up story. He's not a dumb man, Pat. He won't show up yet."

A bleep sounded from her communications board. She leaned backward and pressed a spot on the board. "What is it, Jo?"

"You've got a visitor upstairs."

Kira frowned. "Who?" She didn't get unexpected visitors anymore. She'd withdrawn from her society circles after her father's death. The only visitors she got now were preplanned engagements—or trouble.

"You'll want to see this to believe it," Jo said, no humor in her voice.

Kira hurried from the office, Pat right behind her, to the

wall of vid-screens. She stared mutely at the screen displaying the front door of her family home.

"Either your ex-husband is a lot dumber than you thought," Pat said wryly, "or he's a lot more clever than we guessed."

She glared at Pat, who only shrugged. Then she remembered David. He was standing at the far side of the vid-screens watching her. For a moment, she was caught in his gaze, wondering what he was thinking behind his unreadable expression. Shaking off his scrutiny, she turned back to the vid-screens, trying to concentrate on the business at hand.

Damn David anyway for getting her into this mess with Ennoren. If she were a better leader, she'd wipe his memory. He was a danger to their whole operation, whether he was a spy or not. And it was her responsibility to deal with him. But he'd made it impossible for her to consider harming him in any way. How could she hurt someone she wanted to kiss? Damn him for that, too.

She walked to the communications board across the room and punched in the internal comm-system for the house. "What are you doing here, Eain?" she demanded, watching his face on the screen.

He glanced directly at the vid-scanner and smiled. "Good afternoon, Kira. Did I disturb you?"

"I'm in the bath."

"Alone? Or do you have company?" There was a familiar threat just beneath the seemingly emotionless tone of his voice.

"I've got a string of lovers up here with me," she answered, letting amusement curl into her voice. Without the benefit of a vid-screen on his side of the door, Eain couldn't see her shaking hands or the thin sheen of sweat on her brow. Her voice betrayed none of her fear.

"Open the door, Kira," he snapped, snarling at her through the vid-screen. "We have to talk."

"About what?"

"One of your lovers," he growled.

Kira's stomach clenched. "Which one?" Her voice didn't sound as flippant as she wanted it to.

"Tygran. Raf Tygran."

For just an instant, Kira couldn't breathe. She looked across the room to where Raf stood. He'd entered while she was in her office with Pat. Now he waited with the others by the wall of screens. "Who?" Kira asked, staring into Raf's narrowed blue eyes.

"You know who I'm talking about," Ennoren said, more pleasantly now.

And Kira knew she'd hesitated too long before asking her last question. "I'll be down in a minute." She snapped the comm-link off before she could hear his response, but she didn't miss his smug smile. "Guess our little shootout with the Leeches caught some unneeded attention," Kira said to Raf. "How wanted are you on this planet right now?"

David answered for the pilot. "The commander will arrest him on sight. Actually, since he thinks Tygran's your lover, he may kill him on sight."

His voice drew her gaze, but his last statement made her frown. She opened her mouth to ask what he meant, then closed it again. Explanations could wait. First, she had to deal with her ex-husband. "Okay, Raf. I don't know where you are or what happened to you last night. And you didn't stay in my home." She was already moving toward the door leading to the lifts. "Grainne, is he wearing a detector?"

The red haired girl at the computer block did a quick scan, then indicated that Ennoren was clean.

"Xep," Kira called to the Shifter.

"Problems?"

"Meet me at lift four. I need your help."

"Almost there now."

Kira was stepping through the sliding door toward the lifts when a hand dropped on her shoulder. She turned, meeting David's gaze. And saw a concern that bordered on fear.

"If Ennoren knows about Raf, he may also know I was with you last night. Don't let him think I stayed in your house either, Kira," he warned in an undertone, for her ears only. "And don't let him suspect you've taken me into your bed." When she frowned, he growled, "This is for my benefit as well as yours."

The request confused her, but she didn't have time to think about it then. "Fine," she snapped and headed to the lift that would take her closest to the front door of the mansion. Xep arrived as the doors opened and followed her into the lift without a word.

When she stepped out into the white stone and glass entryway of the mansion she'd grown up in, she was alone, wearing a full-length, black silk robe. The lift doors closed and were hidden by a hologram that blended with the surrounding stone walls. She shook her hair until it felt sufficiently tousled, then approached the door.

Her spine tingled, uncomfortably aware that David was

watching this scene from the command room with the others. Taking a deep breath, she opened the sprawling dark wooden doors. Ennoren stood only inches away, putting him right in her face the second the barrier was removed. He slowly took in her robe and her dry but mussed hair. There was a mixture of angry suspicion and desire in his blue eyes that Kira didn't like.

"State your business, Eain," she challenged without offering to let him in the house.

His mouth tightened. "This will take a few minutes, and I doubt you want your neighbors to see you in such a state in the middle of the afternoon."

"I don't particularly care." She shrugged. "But come in, anyway." She moved aside, leaning against the door as he stepped past her. She shut the doors and without a word sauntered toward a sitting room at the far end of the hall, leaving Ennoren to follow.

The room she took him to was one he'd always hated. It was filled with Navajo rugs and pottery, the colors all cream, rust and turquoise. A number of pillows and a low, cushioned couch surrounded an open fire pit in the middle of the room. Other than the pillows and couch, the room was bare of furniture. Ennoren hated to sit that close to the ground, saying again and again that men were not designed to sit on the floor.

That memory made her cocky smile authentic as she sank easily onto one of the pillows. "Have a seat," she offered, mocking him with her outstretched hand.

Glowering, he perched on the soft arm of the couch, putting most of his weight on his legs to keep from collapsing the cushions.

"Now, what's all this about, Eain? I thought I told you never to come here again."

"This is about the law, Kira. The same law which I am fully aware you've been breaking for…what, four, four and half years now."

"Really? And what specific law is that? The one that says I must see my ex-husband on a regular basis?"

"This isn't about us," he snapped. "It's about the pilot, Tygran."

"He's a pilot! How exciting."

"Kira," Ennoren's voice dropped to a low growl. "You were seen at the Docks with this man. He's wanted by the law on at least seven planets. If you're harboring a fugitive, you'll get ten to life in a hole."

"Harboring a fugitive, hmm? Sounds very noble of me, don't you think?" She shifted, pulling the robe tighter when it began to fall open, and folded her hands in her lap, ignoring Eain's glance at her briefly exposed legs. "Too bad I've never done anything that noble."

"This wouldn't be noble. He's a thief, a smuggler and a murderer."

"Afraid for my life, Eain? That's not at all like you."

He shot from his tentative perch and began pacing the room. "So smug," he hissed beneath his breath. "So damned sure you're right, and your money will buy you anything you want. You think you're above the law?" He whirled on her. "If I find Tygran here, Kira, he's a dead man. And I won't stop the law from falling on you, either."

She sighed and stood. "I would expect nothing less."

He straightened, snapping down the edges of his uniform jacket. "You play innocent so well. Always did. Such a sweet face, such pretty eyes. A man would never guess the deception that hides behind those eyes."

"Eain…"

Before she could finish, Ennoren took two long strides and gripped the lapels of her robe, pulling her flush to his body. "Does your lover pilot know how well you lie, bitch? Or can you deceive even another liar? A man doesn't stand a chance with you. I never did."

"Get your hands off me," she said, her voice even, calm and dangerous.

He loosened one hand only to grip the back of her neck roughly. "Were you ever as innocent as you look? Were you ever innocent at all?" he demanded in a gravel-rough voice.

"Yes." She met his angry, hungry gaze. "I was innocent once. A very long time ago."

As abruptly as he'd grabbed her, he let go, and Kira stumbled backward with the sudden release of tension. He stalked to the door, his spine stiff beneath the crisp lines of his uniform.

"This isn't over, Kira. I'll be back for Tygran. If he's had a taste of you, he won't be far off." He stopped just at the entry to the sitting room and turned to face her again. "By the way, one of my Guards has turned up missing. David Cario. You met him the other day at the blockade."

She nodded.

"Seems he was seen in the Docks last night, too. I'd hate to think one of my men got himself mixed up in something unlawful. Or even got himself killed." He turned away, calling over his shoulder as he walked to the front door, "For a pretty face."

CHAPTER SEVEN

THE WEDDING WAS BEAUTIFUL. MOM AND DAD EVEN MANAGED to be civil to Eian. Eian's father was his usual intimidating self and his mother barely spoke all night, but when I talked to her, she was very happy for Eian and me. The only bad part of the night was when the press showed up. Dad managed to keep them at bay. Given the number of senators who attended the wedding, Eian was grateful for my dad's help. The last thing we wanted was to insult any of the people who can help Eian's career.

We're off to Kyoto Three for our honeymoon. I can't wait. I love Eian so much.

—From the journal of Kira Farseaker

KIRA TOOK A SERIES OF LONG, slow breaths before

heading back to the lift. She shed the robe on the way down, dressing again in her leggings and tunic while Xep shifted back to its natural form.

"Did he hurt you?" she asked, concentrating on a button at the collar of her tunic so she wouldn't have to meet the Shifter's whirling eyes.

"No. But he hurt you?"

"No. He can't hurt me any more, Xep." She straightened but stared at the lift doors, still not looking into Xep's steady gaze.

"He has made this personal. More so now than ever before."

"He's getting desperate. He can't control me, and he can't catch me. I've eluded him and his law for too long. It's making him angry. That's all."

"He thinks David is with you now."

"Yes. But since he probably sent him in the first place, that's not really surprising."

"He mentioned that David might have been killed. Do you think he believes that?"

Kira took a moment to consider the Shifter's question. *"Maybe. That might explain why he came today. If he thought his 'spy' had died before completing the mission..."* She paused. *"Or he was just trying to safeguard David's position here by making it seem as if he wasn't sent as a plant."* She groaned and rubbed her temples as the lift doors opened. *"I don't know, Xep. I just don't know. It's all getting too complicated, and I can't seem to work it out any more."*

A rush of exhaustion stormed through her so that she had to force herself to walk out of the lift.

Xep rested a golden hand on her shoulder as they exited.

"I know this is hard on you, Kira. But you've done well. And it's almost over."

Kira nodded, finally facing the swirls of purple, blue and green that were the Shifter's eyes. *"The time is even closer now, Xep,"* she warned. *"We can't afford any delay. As soon as Pat has the clearance codes, we're on the ship."* She turned back toward Command, the instant flash of exhaustion pushed aside. *"Make sure all the Shifters are ready for a sudden departure. Because we won't be able to come back."*

Command buzzed with chatter and active people. Everything fell silent when she stepped to the center of the room. "All right, everyone, you heard the man. He's coming back, which means we've got next to no time left. Pat, the clearance codes are your top priority—the second you've got a working set, we're on the ship. I don't care what you have to do, but get them a-sap." She turned until she saw Tygran. "Raf, get in touch with your co-pilot and crew. They need to be ready to move at any point within the next two or three days. Any sign that the law or the Leeches have discovered where the ship is?"

"No sign of either," he confirmed.

She had to admire his businesslike tone. "Let's hope it stays that way. The rest of you, make sure all your affairs are taken care of. You've got one last chance to back out. This is a one-way trip. I know you've all thought about it, but think hard one last time. Anyone who wants to stay behind has to leave tonight. We'll arrange the identity changes with the group staying behind."

Kira looked at each of the faces in the room, Shifter and human alike. All were faces she'd known for four and half years, some even longer. Faces of those she'd fought with, and would give her life for. Faces of people she considered members of her family.

She was both proud and sad to see the determination in the human faces, their willingness to give up the planet they'd called home all their lives. Each of the Shifters in the room sent her an unconditional "feel" of certainty also—using that form of direct communication that needed no words to translate. The sensation broke her heart.

"Everyone back to work, then," she ordered, trying to hide the emotion-roughened quality of her voice. "I want to have this place prepared to be shut down, and everything we need ready to load by tomorrow morning." As the buzz of activity began, Kira searched out her second and pulled her aside. "Where's David?"

Jo nodded to a side door that led to the fan rooms—rooms where smoking was allowed within the complex. "He didn't look very happy when he left," Jo said, her violet eyes narrowed, her full mouth pursed. "He seemed to find the conversation you and Ennoren had…upsetting. I couldn't say for sure, Kira, but it came across as jealousy to me."

"Don't be stupid, Jo," Kira snapped, then breathed out her temper. "Sorry. That little scene with Eain left me a bit raw."

"Understandable." Jo patted her shoulder.

"It doesn't matter. I need to talk to David. Will you make sure Raf can get in touch with his crew? And make sure he has all the supplies he needs."

Jo nodded and a familiar gleam lit her eyes. Kira lifted a brow, then shook her head. "Just don't distract him for too long," she warned. "We all need to be ready."

"Me?" Jo was about as good at innocent as she was at

cooking, and Jo was a very bad cook. Kira chuckled and nodded her second away.

She stood staring at the door that led to David, trying to settle herself for another confrontation. The fights and accusations were wearing on her. The exhaustion that had swept her in the lift sat heavily on her shoulders. And dread mixed with a tingling of anticipation at seeing the Guard. Just the thought of his kiss made her lips burn. Knowing she'd remember the feel of his touch all too vividly in his presence, Kira wasn't sure she'd be able to manage this meeting. But it had to be done.

Pushing her hair behind her ears, she left Command. Raf stopped her in the corridor just outside the air-sealed entrance to the fan rooms.

"Kira," he began, then fell silent and stared at the floor for a few minutes, his brow deeply creased with unspoken thoughts. After a time, his brow softened and he grinned. "You're something else, Farseaker. And for what it's worth, I think liars are the best kinds of people."

A laugh burst from Kira so suddenly it surprised her and made her laugh harder. "Glad to know it," she said when she could talk again. "Thanks." She tapped his arm gently. "Now, get off your ass and make sure you're ready to pilot us off this rock."

He smiled, winked and squeezed her shoulder before walking away. Kira shook her head, baffled by the scene but thankful for the release of tension. When she stepped through the air seal into the smoking rooms, she was grinning.

DAVID LEANED AGAINST A WALL, taking a deep drag on his cigarette. He'd seen Kira and Raf's brief exchange—the air seal was transparent—but he hadn't been able to hear them. It didn't matter. Seeing was enough to make his blood boil. Her grin didn't help his state of mind any.

He took another deep pull on the cigarette, waiting for her to notice him. When she did, her step faltered. She slowed, moving toward him with a wary gaze.

"I think there are a few things you'd better explain to me," she said.

Her hard tone made him bristle. "I was going to say the same thing." He puffed at the cigarette again, the glowing tip almost to his fingers. He dropped it to the floor, smashed it beneath his boot heel and lit another.

"Me first," Kira said, ignoring his glare. "What was all that about Ennoren killing Raf if he thought he was my lover?"

"A fact," David answered with a shrug. "The commander would kill him for the simple fact that he was having an affair with you."

Her brow creased. "I doubt that. He might kill Raf, but not because I was having an affair with him." She stopped, her gaze unfocused and turned inward, then quietly said, "Unless he thought it would hurt me. Then he might kill him."

"Would it?"

"What?"

She snapped her gaze back to his face, and David felt the strength of her golden eyes in his every cell. "Would it hurt you if Raf were killed?"

She dismissed the comment with a wave of her hand. "It always hurts me when someone I know gets killed."

"But would Tygran's death hurt you especially?"

She puffed out an impatient breath and paced away. David could see the conversation wasn't going the way she wanted it to. He didn't care. He needed these answers.

"I don't know what the hell you're talking about, David," she said. "And it doesn't matter anyway. I want to know why you didn't want Ennoren to think you were here last night. You tell me I'm keeping you a prisoner—"

"You are."

"But you warn me before I go to talk with your commander," she continued over his interruption, "so that I'll make a specific effort not to mention you." She stopped and turned to face him. "Why? I could have slipped. I could have given away that I knew where you were. He'd have a warrant to search the mansion within minutes if he thought I was keeping you here. Why would you give me a warning you must have known would put me on guard?"

"Why would I want him to know I'm here?" David countered, throwing his half-finished cigarette to the ground and stalking closer to her. "You said you'd release me within the week. Why would I want Ennoren, of all people, to find me here when I know he'd kill me on sight?"

The statement made her gasp. "What…?"

He got in her face. "I told you already. I don't want him to think you've slept with me. He'd kill me for that as easily as he'd kill Raf for it."

"First, why would he assume I'd sleep with you just because you were here?"

"After our meeting at the blockade, he has every reason to suspect that you wanted more from me than conversation."

"Oh! You arrogant son of a bitch," she nearly shouted in indignation.

David grabbed her chin, none too gently, and lifted her face. "Don't dare deny your attraction to me, Kira. There were two of us involved in that kiss in the canteen."

She jerked her head out of his grip and stalked off. "You're as delusional as Ennoren."

She stopped abruptly and David, following close behind her, almost knocked her over. He grabbed her shoulders to balance her, but as soon as she steadied herself, she wrenched away from his touch.

"None of this has anything to do with anything," she spat. "Whether I'm attracted to you or not, whether Raf is my lover or not, has nothing to do with anything. I have less than three days now, and I don't have time for this pettiness. You don't want Ennoren to find you here? Fine! He won't. I've got—"

David grabbed her shoulders again and hauled her close. "Is he?"

"What?" she demanded.

"Is Raf Tygran your lover?"

Her mouth dropped open. "I can't believe you're still…" She expelled a disbelieving breath, shook her head and shoved away from him.

She started to walk off again, but David kept pace with her easily. "Answer the question, Kira."

"It's none of your goddamned business!"

His arm dropped like a bolt against the steel-plated wall beside her, stopping her retreat. She turned, her golden-eyed gaze sparking like lava. Her breath came in deep, angry heaves that made her chest rise and fall sharply. And David felt his blood reaching critical heat. "I'm making it my goddamned business," he answered, his voice low and rough. "Are you having an affair with Tygran?"

She lowered her gaze and pushed against the arm that blocked her retreat. "I don't have time for affairs," she mumbled. "With anyone."

He gripped the back of her neck, barely maintaining his control against the storming desire riding through him. Forcing her head around, he tilted her face up, bringing her lips only a breath away from his. "Make time," he whispered hoarsely, then covered her mouth with a hard, desperate kiss.

She stiffened under his assault. Her hands came up to his chest, and David knew she would push him away despite the increased pressure he reflexively put on the back of her neck. But even if she tried, he didn't think he could let her go.

Then she melted.

The utter cessation of resistance staggered him. Her hands against his chest convulsed into fists in his shirt, and she pressed against him. He pulled her closer with one arm wrapped around her waist, the other dropping from her neck to her upper back. The eager sweetness of her kiss tumbled through him, bringing his already needy body to full, hard readiness.

He slid his hand from her shoulders to her bottom, squeezing hard. She moaned low in her throat, and David urged her hips firmly against his throbbing erection. God, she tasted good. He moved her back against the wall, pressing her against it, freeing his hands to cover her breasts. She dropped her head as far as the wall would allow and arched her back when he squeezed roughly at the soft, tender mounds.

The groan she released as his mouth worked down the column of her throat made his grip tighten, and her fingers dug into his shoulders in response. He shoved aside the edge of her vest and settled his lips against the straining peak of one breast through the material of her tunic. He sucked gently at first, flicking the tip teasingly with his tongue. The helpless moans of pleasure falling from her parted lips nearly drove him mad. His lips grew more persistent, pulling and nipping until she began to shake.

He returned hungrily to her mouth, devouring her with hot and urgent kisses.

"David."

His name sighed out of her, and he swallowed the passion and need in her voice. "God, Kira, I want you." He raked her neck with his mouth again before moving to torment the soft flesh of her ear. "Now." He knew he was losing control, knew he'd take her in the corridor against the wall if he didn't get them into a room soon. He didn't notice the push of her hands on his chest until her voice broke through the haze of his desire.

"David, stop."

He pulled back enough to look into her face, but he didn't release her. Her face was flushed, her hair a sexy mess, her breathing rapid and shallow.

"I can't do this." She shoved harder against him until he took a step back and dropped his arms to his sides.

His eyes narrowed. "You were doing this just fine a moment ago."

Her cheeks flushed deeper. "I can't...I don't have the

time," she mumbled and before he could stop her, she moved beyond his reach. "I'm sorry, David," she whispered, golden eyes wide. She walked away, her back stiff, her gait slow but determined.

He could catch her. He could reach her in a few strides and take her back into his arms again, make her forget time, her mission, Raf Tygran, even Ennoren. But he didn't. He stood and watched her walk away, working to steady his own breathing, to relax his tensed muscles.

She might have just saved them both from a terrible mistake. But he wasn't happy about being saved.

CHAPTER EIGHT

I'M REALLY STARTING TO WORRY ABOUT MOM AND DAD. THEY'VE gotten involved in the extermination debate—publicly supporting the Shifters. Dad says SCR has lied about Shifter nature, that they're not dangerous. Eian says my dad is deluded. I'm not really sure who to believe anymore—my husband who's on the front line of the exterminations, or my parents who are so adamant in their beliefs.

What I do know is that I can't have them in the same room now without a full-blown argument taking place. Eian doesn't even want me talking to my parents. To keep the peace, I don't go home often. But I'm really worried about them. Some of the people who claim to be Shifter supporters are dangerous.

—From the journal of Kira Farseaker

KIRA CLOSED the sliding door to her bedroom in the compound, then sank against it. She'd taken to sleeping down in the compound instead of in the mansion as soon as the complex had been livable. There were too many memories up in the house. Memories that came back to haunt her now.

She ran her hands through her hair and stared up at the ceiling, her heart still pounding with the desire David had so quickly sparked. God, but she wanted him. She couldn't remember a man ever doing this to her, confusing her and exciting her at the same time. Ennoren had never turned her into a quivering, boneless heap with only a kiss.

Except that was more than a kiss, she thought ruefully. She'd very nearly let David take her in the blasted corridor. With a groan, she pushed away from the wall's support and walked to her bed, sprawling face-first on the soft mattress. David was supposed to be the enemy, she told her errant mind. He was almost certainly Ennoren's spy. He already knew more about the complex, about her, than was safe. He was supposed to be her prisoner, for Christ's sake.

She rolled onto her back, pressed the palms of her hands into her aching eyes. What was she doing? She was supposed to be a leader. She was supposed to be getting the Shifters off this planet before they were completely destroyed. She didn't have time for affairs.

She hadn't had time for much of anything in the last five years. Not since the detector plant was bombed. No, she corrected, time had become her enemy almost a year before that, just after her parents were killed. The thought of her parents—a father who'd raised her for several years all by himself after her birth mother's death, a stepmother who'd loved her as if she'd given birth to her—brought on a dull ache that never completely went away.

She'd clung to Eain for months after they'd been killed. They were caught in the wrong place at the wrong time, according to the official report—walked into the middle of a protest against the exterminations just as a riot broke out. The Guard claimed the riot was started by the protestors. For months, Kira found no reason to disbelieve the official reports.

Until she discovered the private log her father had left her. A log that documented his and his wife's fight against the exterminations, both publicly and privately. God, she'd been naïve. She'd never even guessed. She knew they spoke out publicly against the exterminations, but she never suspected the extent to which they'd struggled.

Their deaths weren't an accident, either.

She never got proof, of course. Only the warnings in her father's log, the suspicions. The distrust of Ennoren. And the fear for her. Her father had gone to great lengths just before he was killed to make sure that no matter what, Ennoren couldn't get his hands on the Farseaker family fortune. He ensured his daughter would always have that safety net. She could only marvel at her father's foresight and be grateful for it.

Lifting the pocket-comm from her vest pocket, she flicked a switch. "Gregor, Op. three, level five." A quiet, powerful song began to play, the opening full of percussion and the deep accompaniment of an oboe.

She toyed with the idea of requesting food, then changed her mind. The others had better things to do than cater to her. She had better things to do too, but she couldn't face anyone just yet. Her body was still tingling and restless. She could make a new journal entry; she hadn't had much time for her journal over the last few months. But what would she say? That she was confused and exhausted? She doubted the journal would help her solve her problems. She was tempted to go up to the mansion, to hide in her father's study. But that wouldn't solve anything, either.

The most pressing problem was the clearance code to get off-planet. Pat said Ennoren had updated the approval and verification procedures. Did Ennoren know they would try to get off-planet? Did he know time was running out for both of them? Her temples throbbed to the beat of the horn solo that built the tempo of the music. Never enough time, she thought wistfully. Not enough time with her parents. Not enough time for the Shifters. Not enough time for friends.

And not enough time for lovers.

But there would be, she told herself firmly, after they escaped Ennoren's watchful eye. After they reached Kierna'Rhoan, she'd have all the time in the universe for friends and family and lovers. Except the man she wanted—more than any other man—wouldn't be coming with them.

It was ridiculous to feel that way so soon. She barely knew David. Yet she'd never felt this kind of desire for any of the men in her group, men she'd worked with and fought beside for years. Men who would be traveling with her to Kierna'Rhoan. David had broken through a barrier she'd held firmly in place since her divorce, and she couldn't undo that now. Unfortunately, that left her facing the possibility of a very lonely future.

She pushed the thought aside, forced her mind away from David and his intense passion, away from the melancholy memories of her parents and away from her broodings over what Ennoren knew and what he didn't. With a curt word, she ordered the music off and stood. She straightened her vest, went to the pull-down sink and splashed cold water on her face, dried it and ran her fingers through her hair.

She confronted the mirror above the sink and barely recognized the woman who looked back. Hard eyes with faint circles beneath them, mouth tense and frowning. Nothing like the young girl Ennoren had seduced into marriage, the girl whose innocence he'd shattered. She appeared hard now, unrelenting, determined and much too world-wise.

"But then, we can't stay innocent forever," she told her reflection. "Innocents don't know that there are bad things that have to be stopped."

And, she thought as she flicked on her pocket-comm and requested Pat, she had several bad things to stop.

DAVID WANDERED THE FAN ROOMS, working his way at a steady rate through the pack of cigarettes he'd been given. It wasn't until he was on his last one that he noticed what he was doing. He stared at the unlit stick for a long time, brooding silently over this unfortunate circumstance. He was about to light it anyway, when a shape stepped through a nearby air seal.

This was the first person he'd seen in an hour. He scowled, hoping whoever it was would find themselves someplace else to be. He wasn't that lucky. The man walked toward him without hesitancy. He was a thin man, of average height and build, with gold-blond hair and dark blue eyes. His face was soft, almost feminine but for the squaring of jaw and the faint stubble on his chin.

"I think we should talk, David Cario," the man said in a strange, whispery voice that left David feeling mildly uncomfortable.

"Do I know you?"

The man smiled. "You can call me Xep, if you like. And no, we haven't been formally introduced."

"Listen, Xep, I'm not really in the mood for an interrogation right now, okay?" David lit his cigarette.

Xep glanced at the glowing tip of the cigarette, at the smoke curling up from its end. His soft features furrowed in a frown. "I'm not fond of cigarette smoke," he said when he noticed David's questioning stare. "But no matter. I need to speak with you, so I'll deal with it. Shall we have a seat?" He nodded to a side room and a row of couches.

David inclined his head but let the man lead the way into the room. When Xep sat, David continued to stand, legs braced apart, arms crossed over his chest, defiantly puffing at the cigarette.

Xep shrugged. "I would like to discuss Kira with you."

"Why?" David shot out before he could stop himself.

The slight rise of Xep's gold eyebrows made David snarl inwardly at his own loss of control where that woman was concerned.

"Kira would like nothing better than to trust you," Xep said, sitting too straight in the deep couch. "She sees something in you that seems to surpass your position with Ennoren's Guard."

"Does she? Did she tell you that?"

Xep shook his head. "She doesn't have to. I'm not even sure she knows it consciously. I've known Kira for many years now. She's a remarkable woman. Strong and vulnerable and caring. She's done a lot for the Shifters—more than she should have."

"You sound like you don't like Shifters."

The man chuckled. "I can't help but like them. But that's not what I'm here to discuss. I'm here because of Kira. And you."

"What about me? You don't know me."

"I know more of you than you might think. I know of your passion for Kira. I also know that you're lying to her. And I know that you're lying to Commander Ennoren."

David dropped his arms to his side, stunned. The cigarette in his mouth hung perilously from his lips, but he barely noticed. "What are you talking about?"

"I knew your sister, David Cario."

The blow was more than David could take standing up. He landed heavily on one of the couches and stared at Xep. His cigarette fell to the metal floor but he ignored it. "Who are you?" he breathed. "How did you know her?"

"Tina Cario was one of those remarkable humans whom I've had the privilege to meet in my lifetime. She was passionate also, like you. Like Kira. She was a good person."

"Who are you?" David repeated.

And as he watched, the man before him melted and folded and changed until a golden, bright-eyed Shifter sat in his place. In the next instant, the man was back, returning David's gaze steadily.

"You aren't telepathic like your sister was, so this form is necessary for communication."

"Telepathic?" David whispered vaguely. The conversation he'd been having and the change he just witnessed refuted everything the government said about Shifters. It also seemed to confirm a lot of what his sister had told him six years ago.

"In our natural state, that is the only way we can communicate with humans. Even then, it was some time before we could master your word-based language. The concept was not altogether unfamiliar to us," Xep assured him with an earnest gaze. "It's just been many, many generations since we found it necessary to communicate using words as representations of complex thought and emotion."

"You're not supposed to be able to communicate," David told the man-thing before him. "Mimic, yes; think and speak on your own, no."

Xep smiled sadly. "I thought, between Kira and Tina, you wouldn't believe those falsified studies anymore." He sighed. "Well, perhaps we can change your mind yet. Tina once told me you were too stubborn for your own good." The creature settled back into the couch, deep blue eyes steady on David's face. "You have questions for me, I see."

"Was she one of them?" David burst out before he could talk himself out of asking. "Was Tina one of the ones responsible for the bombing?"

Xep tilted his head, his blue eyes blinked. "Can't you guess the answer? She was your sister, a good woman. Don't you know her well enough to answer that question yourself?"

"She was convicted." David's gaze turned inward, his head reeling with memories and guilt. "They said there was evidence, but… But she was executed before I could get to her, before I could tell her…" His voice dropped off, choking on the years-old pain.

"Ennoren executed her," Xep stated in his quiet voice.

"Yes." David snarled. "He told me the evidence was irrefutable."

"But you didn't believe him. Still don't?"

"I…I didn't at first." David pulled his thoughts back together, tried to regain his composure and control. But he couldn't look into Xep's eyes when he said, "I believe now."

"No, you don't, David. Not entirely. But that's the lie you hope he believes. Is that why he allowed you into his company? Because he thought you'd accepted your sister's supposed crimes? Or is it so that he can keep you under his watchful eye?"

David stood and paced the room. "You a mind reader, Xep?" he ground out. He'd spent years developing and maintaining the facade of belief in the story Ennoren had fed him. Years earning his way into the man's trust enough to be transferred to his elite command. And in moments, this man, this Shifter had toppled his control, broken his facade and uncovered his lies.

"I can," the Shifter said, "but I don't. But your non-word thoughts—they're very hard for you to control and too easy for us to read, especially when you're upset. You give yourselves away very easily to us sometimes. It surprises me how often humans can fool each other with their word lies." Xep shrugged. "It's of no consequence. I won't be giving you away to Commander Ennoren, now, will I?"

The teasing smile that Xep gave him made David stop to stare at the Shifter. The damned thing was right. David had been worried that he was uncovered, that Ennoren would know of his deceit now. But from whom? A Shifter who would bring about his own death sentence if he approached the commander?

The realization stole his nervous energy, and he collapsed onto a couch again, studying the Shifter with a new appreciation. They weren't supposed to be logical, either, he thought ruefully. So much for scientific evidence. "Okay," he said with a deep breath. "So you won't give me away to the commander. What do you want from me? Why are you telling me all of this?"

Xep frowned and glanced at the black rug in the center of the room. "Therein lies the problem. What I want from you is a guarantee that you're not going to hurt Kira. But I won't ask that of you. Not yet. I also want to know that you're the man I think you are. But how would you prove it?"

Xep looked into his eyes again, and David felt as if he were being pulled into a whirl of colors, though the man's eyes seemed to remain blue.

"What I want from you, David Cario," Xep said very softly, "is for you to understand why Kira does what she does, why it is vital that Ennoren not be allowed to stop us. It's not my place to tell you everything, but perhaps…"

After a quiet moment while David continued to be sucked into the Shifter's gaze, Xep said, "May I tell you a story, David?"

CHAPTER NINE

EIAN FINALLY GOT HIS PROMOTION! HE'S COMMANDER Ennoren now. All those dinner parties we've been hosting have paid off. Eian was right to insist I make every detail perfect.

The only problem is, he's in charge of an extermination squadron now. I'm not so sure how I feel about that part.

—From the journal of Kira Farseaker

IT WAS NEARLY midnight before Kira returned to her small bedroom. Her evening had been busy arranging supplies for Tygran's ship, collecting the funds to pay the smuggler, and overseeing the breakdown of the complex. There was still a day's worth of work to do, but everyone was exhausted. And

Pat was still two days away from getting a working clearance code. At the earliest.

She stripped off her clothing and sank onto her bed with a groan of exhaustion, but her mind was working too fast to sleep. She was too wound up to shut off. They'd seen nothing more of Ennoren that day, but his threat to return loomed heavily over the complex. Her home was most likely being watched, but that didn't affect the movements of the people beneath. There was no more on the newscasts about the missing Guard, one way or the other. Apparently, Ennoren had managed to quash that story's momentum.

But the problem remained: what to do about David? Thoughts of his dark eyes, firm mouth and rough touch made her stomach squirm and her legs jerk restlessly against the mattress. She felt her body readying for him without her permission. She'd sent James to find him and show him to a more comfortable room sometime that evening—she'd lost track of the time. Now she couldn't help wondering where he was in the complex. The compulsion to seek him out was almost overpowering.

"Grrr." She pushed herself out of bed. She wasn't going to get any sleep this way. And she doubted very much if a cold shower would help. Instead, she decided to do something she hadn't done in a very long time.

She pulled on a long, black robe—the very robe Xep had imitated earlier that day—and, out of habit, tucked her pocket-comm into the robe's deep side pocket. Then she left the room, walking on bare feet down the corridor toward the lifts.

Her father's study had been her sanctuary since she was a

little girl. She'd gone there whenever she needed a safe place to think: after her mother's death, just before her father's new marriage, on the first morning before starting at a new school, after her disastrous first date. Always this room had been like a warm hug, a soft voice, a comforting hand running down her hair.

She'd avoided the study for a long time now. Memories clung to the oak-paneled walls and deep blue carpets. Her father's desk still held his old-fashioned pen and ink set, and an antique blotter made of Earth cedar. But it wasn't the memories of her father that had kept her from his study. It was the memory of running here, hiding here after the executions.

The trials had been a farce. The people, some of them little more than children, convicted of bombing the detector plant had all proclaimed their innocence. Another group of militants, the Golden Order, took credit for the bombing later, though no proof had emerged to support their claims. But by that time, it was already too late to save the sacrificed.

And her husband was the one who callously, easily murdered those people in a public spectacle designed to horrify the masses and strengthen the Guard's hold. Those faces had followed her into this room five years ago. And it was here that she'd made up her mind to divorce Ennoren and to use her money toward something good—to help a new friend she'd meet a few months earlier.

The study was still a safe place for her, but the faces of those murdered, and the faces of those lost since, came to her here sometimes. Not always. But often enough that she made fewer visits. When she pushed open the thick wooden doors that night, however, the familiar and comfortable room was free of specters. The faint scent of her father's cologne and wood smoke filled her nostrils and warmed her heart.

She went to the computer board hidden behind an old tapestry depicting another event in the life of Nathaniel Farseaker. She keyed in the replay, set it for holographic emission and sat down in her father's large leather chair to watch his image light the center of the room, recording the events of his days. She smiled when her stepmother interrupted the log entry by sidling into the picture and pinching him on the rear. The entry stopped there and started again several hours later.

Caught up in the comfortable cadence of her father's voice, she didn't hear the door open.

"Kira?"

The soft voice was familiar, but different.

"Xep?" She turned to see the Shifter in human form—male human this time, though she noted with a grin that it had added facial hair to make the male shape more "masculine".

"Are you all right?" the man with Xep's voice asked, coming a few steps into the room and studying her with deep blue eyes. The room was mostly dark, lit only by the light of the holographic picture playing out in the center of the room.

"I'm fine, Xep. Just too tired to sleep." She smiled wanly. "What are you doing up here? And in human form?"

Xep stepped back to the door and motioned someone from the corridor into the room. "I thought you two should talk." The Shifter walked out of the room before Kira could protest the intrusion.

David stood in his black pants and turtleneck just inside the doorway, staring at her with hooded eyes, keeping his thoughts private. She rose, clenching the lapels of her robe together. His gaze flicked to the hologram, and Kira ordered it off with a sharp word.

"Lights," she said, more quietly this time, "dim." She blinked as a low, yellow glow like candlelight rose in the room.

"That's the robe you had on earlier," David murmured, his gaze sliding down her body and back to her face. "Do you keep it up here?"

"That was Xep earlier," she said, keeping a hand on the upper lapels. "I didn't have time to go down and get my real robe, and I'd told Ennoren I was in the bath."

He frowned then, walking farther into the room. "You let the Shifter cover you? Without anything else on?"

The strange suspicion on his face made her relax a bit. A slight smile replaced her scowl. "Did you know," she asked in a conversational tone, "that Shifters are asexual? The species isn't divided into male and female or any variation of gender." She offered David a seat on a couch near the room's single curtained window. She hesitated between sitting in her father's chair again or on the couch with David, then gave in to the temptation to be closer to David.

"When they shift into human form, of course," she continued, dropping onto the opposite end of the small couch, "they have to take either male or female forms, but they're as likely to shift to male as female. Some prefer male human shape or female human shape, but it doesn't have anything to do with their own sexuality."

"You know a lot about the Shifters," he said in his husky voice, a crooked smile replacing the suspicion of moments ago. "A lot more than the scientists seem to."

"The scientists—" she sneered at the word, "—never bothered to ask the Shifters. Besides, they were paid to report certain things, whether those things were true or not."

He nodded and looked down at his hands where they rested on his thighs. Against her will, Kira followed his gaze. Then she wished she hadn't. The urge to run her fingers up those muscled thighs stole her breath. Her heart pounded, speeding with the desire to touch him. She jerked her gaze back to his face, but not in time to avoid being discovered. David watched her face in a way that made her stomach jump and her cheeks warm.

"Why did Xep think we should talk?" she asked, feigning a casual, authoritative demeanor. Her act didn't fool either of them.

"He seems to think that there are some things in my past I should tell you about. And some things you'd want to tell me."

He didn't move closer, but Kira could almost feel his touch as he studied her face, brazenly letting his gaze wander down the front of her body to the white patch of her legs exposed by the parted hem of the robe. "What things?" Her breathing was unsteady, making her voice sound whispery and rough. She cleared her throat and asked again in what she hoped was a firmer tone. "What things in your past?"

David met her gaze again. "My sister, Tina. She was one of the people convicted of bombing the detector plant five years ago. One of the people your ex-husband, and my boss, executed."

Kira felt like she'd been kicked in the stomach. Her breath rushed out in a painful gasp. And all at once, her sanctuary was haunted again. She closed her eyes tight against the images, only vaguely aware that a tear slipped past one eyelid and down her cheek. She jumped, startled into opening her eyes, when she felt a hand on her jaw. She looked into the depths of David's black eyes and her guilt at keeping him prisoner was irrationally doubled.

"Oh God, David, I'm sorry," she whispered. "I'm so sorry."

He ran the pad of his thumb over her cheekbone and shook his head. "No. I didn't tell you that to make you feel bad, Kira. You weren't responsible. Ennoren was. My sister. And me. But not you."

"They didn't do it." Kira gripped the hand on her cheek. "None of them. They'd been working for a group…a group like this one, trying to hide and save the Shifters from extinction. They weren't radicals. The group didn't believe in violence—especially killing others." Whoever had planted the bomb had set it to go off at night when most people were out of the building. Unfortunately, the timer misfired and the bomb went off in the middle of a work day, killing hundreds. The severity of the death toll gave Ennoren leeway to speed up the conviction process, and very few people bothered to question the guilt of those executed.

"I know," David said, soothing and gentle. "I've known for a long time now that she wasn't guilty. But…there were always doubts, Kira. I've never had any proof that she didn't help plant that bomb. Only gut instinct and a few secondhand testimonies."

He moved back against the couch arm, took a deep breath

and stared up at the ceiling. "I was working undercover in the Docks when the bombing happened."

"Undercover?"

He glanced down at her, a mildly amused grin curving his mouth. "You honestly think the Guards let the Docks go totally unchecked?"

"No." Kira shrugged, realizing how obvious that should have been. "I suppose not. But your records never—" She stopped short, realizing too late she'd said too much.

David breathed out what was almost a chuckle. "Checked my records?"

She nodded, lifting her chin despite the heat rising in her cheeks.

"The records of all undercover operatives are…altered as a matter of procedure. Just in case." His faint smile was wry. "I believe mine had me working vice before I joined Ennoren's squad." He paused, looking down at the space of couch between them.

"It's not an easy job," he murmured, "undercover in the Docks. There's a lot of…information. A lot of temptations. They hand-pick the people that are sent in. I come from a long line of Naravan Guards, and before that, soldiers and police on Earth. And I had a record for being incorruptible." He snorted at the label.

The self-mocking gesture made her flinch.

"You learn things in the Docks though," he continued. "I knew what my sister was involved in. But she was my sister. I couldn't turn her in. And I wasn't working under Ennoren's command at the time. It was his job, his squad, that handled the Shifters and Shifter support terrorist groups."

"It is your job now," Kira said in a quiet, cautious voice. "You work for him."

He met her gaze with hard, unreadable eyes. "I've reasons for that, too."

Kira tried to absorb what he was telling her, but something seemed wrong, unsaid. And it was the still-unsaid that left her wary. He turned away, focusing on the tapestry on the wall opposite the couch, ignoring her speculative stare.

"My parents learned about Tina, also. They'd both been Guards. But, like me, they couldn't turn her over to Ennoren. They stopped talking to her, though—disowned her in a way I couldn't. But then, I was never around. For as often as I actually talked to Tina, I might as well have been a stranger. When we did talk, we fought—mostly about the Shifters. Word reached me in the Docks that the detector plant had been bombed. The news was barely spread before we heard about the convictions."

He stopped, swallowing audibly. "By the time I reached Capital, the executions had been carried out. So quick," he breathed. "Ennoren showed me the proof."

"And you believed him?" Kira found herself whispering.

David looked back into her eyes, silent for what seemed a long time. Then, very quietly, he said, "Yes. And no." He stood and crossed to the tapestry, studying the image of Nathaniel Farseaker, keeping his back to her. "My parents, they've never been the same. They won't talk about her or say her name. They try to pretend she never existed. But the loss is obvious. She was only twenty-two."

Kira followed him as far as the desk. She didn't know whether to comfort him or not, whether he would reject her efforts or appreciate them. This man, a man who worked for her ex-husband, whom she had every reason to distrust, was telling her that he had as much reason to hate Ennoren as she did. Maybe more. But he'd been under Ennoren's command for three years now. And the one thing she could say about her ex-husband was that he was very careful about the people he allowed to work in his squad.

With his back still to her, David said, "Xep tells me the executions were what caused you to divorce him."

"They were the final brick in the wall that had grown between Eain and me." She leaned her hip against the desk and toyed with her father's pen. "But there were other things before that, other reasons why I wouldn't have been able to stay with him long."

"When did you meet Xep?"

"A few months before the…before I filed for divorce. Why?"

"He knew Tina. He said you have the same kind of passion she did."

Kira set the pen down, frowning. "I didn't when I first met Xep. I was, in a lot of ways, the perfect wife to Ennoren. Quiet, pliable, easily manipulated, easily cowed. Some of that was an act in the end. But after my parents were killed, I was so shattered, I clung to Ennoren."

"Xep told me about your parents' death. They were killed during a riot at a protest against the exterminations."

"I thought I'd lost just about everything when that happened. Except my husband. He was still there, in a way. Eain became my world. And then Xep changed my world forever."

David turned then. "Are you in love with Xep?"

The question made her chuckle. "I love Xep as if I were part of the line—one of Xep's relations. But that's all. Like I said, the Shifters are asexual. Xep understands human attraction and sexual relationships but only in an academic sense."

He nodded and looked at his feet. "He said the same thing." He glanced up and mumbled, "Sorry. It's just hard for me to imagine why you do all this."

"You mean, why Tina did all this?"

"Yes. I still don't fully understand, Kira. And that's a problem for me. I don't understand why she had to do what she did—to the point that it cost her her life. What good is she to the Shifters now?"

"All we can do is follow what we believe is best. We take the risks. It's our right." She stood away from the desk. "Why are you telling me all of this? What do you think I can do for you?"

"I don't know that you can do anything for me. When I found out you were Ennoren's ex-wife, I hoped you'd have the proof I need to clear my sister's name."

"I don't."

He nodded. "I know that now. You wouldn't still be hiding from the law if you had proof against Ennoren."

"Then?"

He closed the space between them in three slow steps, giving her time to retreat. Time she didn't take advantage of. Circling one arm around her waist, he pulled her against his chest and, for a minute, simply held her there.

"I want your trust," he murmured. "I want you to believe that I won't turn you over to him. I'll keep your secret even if you let me leave. I have as much to lose as you do."

"I...I don't trust that easily, David," she breathed. Her

entire being was aware of him, the hard muscles of his body pressed against her, the feel of his hand at the small of her back, the spicy scent of soap he'd used that evening, even the faint hint of cigarette smoke that clung to his clothes.

"Neither do I, Kira."

"Is that the only reason you're here? Is that what you want me to believe? That you followed me to the Docks because you wanted my help with the circumstances surrounding your sister's death?"

"That is partly the reason I tracked you. But not the only reason. I couldn't stop thinking about you after we met." He lowered his mouth to hers, paused, giving her the chance to stop him. When she didn't, he kissed her. His lips worked slowly against hers at first, then he teased her lips apart with his tongue and plunged into her. His kiss was hard, deep and demanding.

And Kira returned that kiss with a heat she didn't recognize in herself. Overpowering need washed over her, through her. The need to be close to him, the need to feel his touch, to comfort and give. And take. The need to lose control—just this once, just for this instant. She wrapped her arms around his neck and twisted her hands into his thick hair. He pulled her closer, tightening his grip almost painfully on her waist, and she reveled in that show of strength and possession.

They clung to each other, their kisses hard and dangerous, their hands urgently exploring lines and curves still hidden beneath their cloths. Beneath the onslaught, she began to tremble.

"Kira."

She heard an echo of her own desperation in his rough, breathless voice.

"Don't pull back now," he said gruffly against her neck. "Give us tonight."

He dropped hot, moist kisses along her neck, in the hollow of her throat, at the base of her jaw, just beneath her ear. Kira moaned, helpless and too desperate to pull away now. She needed him tonight, needed to feel this passion.

But not in her father's study.

"David…" She pushed against his shoulders. He tightened his grip and covered her mouth brutally, refusing to let her talk. She turned her head and managed to speak, though her voice was shaky. "Not in here. I've a better place."

Her words, and the fact that they weren't a refusal, brought his gaze to hers. His already dark eyes were black in the dim lighting, glittering with a desire that staggered her. With effort, she loosened his grip, took one hand and led the way from the study.

She followed the well-remembered corridor, turned down a second hall, and stepped down the four steps that led to her own suite of rooms in the house. She had a small library and computer center in one room. A room full of memories— pictures, schoolwork and degrees, toys from childhood, all the things her father couldn't bring himself to discard. Another room was set aside for painting and music—neither of which she'd much talent for, but her passion for both tended to transcend her lack of skill. Near the rear of her suite was a dressing and cleaning chamber, where her extensive wardrobe remained hermetically sealed to protect the fabric of clothing she no longer had use for.

And set in a corner of the house so that the three walls of windows gave a panoramic view of the estate and the nearby sea, was the bedroom Kira had abandoned many years ago.

After she'd married Eain, she'd moved to his home, but this had been her bed when she returned for visits. She hadn't spent the night here since the complex had been completed, but everything was kept clean and neat by the cleaning droids.

Sliding panels were closed over the wall windows and skylight. A simple word command opened both, revealing the deep, crystalline beauty of the late night. Both Narava's moons hung in the sky—Rupach just at the horizon, huge and yellow, and Lonrach overhead, shining pearly light into the heart of the room. At one corner, a rock-and plant-covered waterfall tinkled quietly. From the small pond at the fall's base, a thin stream meandered through the room before disappearing beneath the stone floor. Thick rugs covered paths across the floor. In the light, these rugs looked like blue-green grass, thick and soft. Her bed frame was carved of the same rock as her small waterfall, decorated with mythical images hidden within real vines of ivy and fragrant flowers.

She led David close to the bed before turning to see his face. He seemed completely unaware of the wealth surrounding him, the money it took to maintain, to build a place such as this on Narava. His dark eyes were focused entirely on her face, and the sheer heat in his expression stole Kira's breath.

"God, you're beautiful," he murmured. One trembling hand touched her cheek. "You glow in this light."

He cupped her cheek gently, and without breaking eye contact, tugged open the sash of her robe with his free hand. The silk parted, washing her skin in moonlight and the humid warmth of the room. She shrugged her shoulders, letting the robe fall in a heap to the floor. His gaze swept down her lean frame, then locked on her face.

The hand he'd used to untie her sash had dropped to his side. Kira lifted his hand and pressed his palm against the center of her chest, letting him feel her hammering heartbeat. She turned her face, kissing the palm of the hand still on her cheek, and slid his other hand over her heated skin to cover her breast. She looked back into his eyes, read the hunger, and pulled his face to hers until their lips were a whisper apart.

"Make this last, David," she murmured. "Please."

He answered with a kiss that was so deeply passionate and so unbearably tender it shook her to the center of her soul.

"I'll give you anything you want tonight, Kira. Everything you need."

He wrapped his arms around her, enveloping her in his heat and his scent. The tantalizing mix of spicy soap and tobacco that clung to his clothes and skin filled her, teasing her beyond thought.

She needed to be closer, to feel all of him, to taste the salt on his skin. Pulling his shirt from his pants, she tugged it over his head when he moved enough to allow its removal. She dropped a kiss onto his chest, then slid her lips slowly over his tensed muscles, her tongue teasing and tasting his flesh. His deep-throated groan made her stomach tighten with feminine satisfaction. He dug his hands into her hair, dropping his head back as her lips closed over his nipple. But he didn't allow her to explore for long. Gently but insistently, he pulled her mouth to his.

"This won't last long if you do much more of that," he murmured harshly against her mouth.

She couldn't prevent the smug smile that curved her lips and narrowed her eyes. He obliterated the smugness with his next devouring kiss. Before Kira realized his hands had moved, he wrapped his arms low around her waist and lifted her off her feet, backing her to the bed.

"Lie down," he urged as he set her on the edge of the bed.

She obeyed without a word. He removed the rest of his clothing and crawled up next to her. Kira's mouth parted at the sight of him. In the silvery glow of moonlight, he looked far more chiseled and lean than she'd thought. All muscle and sinew and lightly tanned flesh. Each movement radiated strength tempered by control. She decided in one giddy instant of irrational thought that Xep could learn a lot about "masculinity" from David. And then David's mouth was on hers, kissing her, and thought gave way to hunger and sensation.

He was true to his word, giving her everything she wanted, all she could take and more, until Kira felt as if she would split in half. With hands and mouth he pushed her, toppled her over the edge of climax twice. And then he took her farther.

She shuddered with reaction, certain she could take no more, when he entered her at last. Her body convulsed around him, and she groaned at the exquisite feel of him inside her. He tensed, remaining still for a long moment, his breath ragged against her throat. When she relaxed a little, he began to move.

For the first time in years, time ceased to have meaning for Kira. She was lost in the mind-blowing, body-rending pleasure David gave her. She couldn't form words, only whimpers, groans and cries of agonized ecstasy amid the torrent of sensations assaulting her flesh. When his rhythmic thrusts grew harder and faster, when his groans turned wild, when his body began to shudder and convulse inside her and around her, Kira cried out in her final, explosive release.

Her mind was slow to return to her surroundings. For long minutes, she swam in a silent world of bliss and exhaustion. Then the sound of the small waterfall reasserted itself. With it came the sound of David's ragged breathing, the feel of him heavy and warm on top of her, the hammering of his heartbeat against her breast, the smell of flowers, musk, sweat and sex, and the subtle glow of moonlight. She took in all of this a piece at a time, unwilling and unable to move, concentrating on slowing her breathing.

When she could lift her heavy arms again, she wrapped them around his neck and pressed her cheek against his. He lifted his weight from her, gazing into her eyes with a look of wonder. Then he moved off her, and she shivered at the sudden loss of warmth. He kicked at the now-tousled blankets until he could cover both of them. She rolled to her side to see him levered up on one elbow, staring down at her. She raised her eyebrows in question, not sure if her voice worked yet.

He answered the unspoken question with a slight smile. "I could use a cigarette now."

Kira chuckled. "Sorry. I don't smoke."

"I know," he murmured, and gathered her into his arms.

She allowed herself to indulge in the feelings of contentment and security his embrace gave her. For as long as she could, she refused to think of consequences, or time, or the control she'd given over to David so eagerly. But the real world wouldn't let her forget it for long.

She shifted in his arms, lifting her face to catch and hold his dark gaze. "This doesn't change anything, David," she murmured. His eyes hardened at those words and his jaw clenched. Before he could talk, she rushed on. "Please understand. I would like nothing better than to give you the trust you ask for. But I can't. I can't allow myself to trust you simply because you've asked me to. Too many lives are in my hands. This isn't just about us."

He sucked in a deep breath and looked past her shoulder to the glass wall beyond. His lips pursed, making the silvery scar on his jaw jump. He pulled one arm away from her, resting it on his waist, and the arm beneath her neck relaxed against the bed. Kira squeezed her eyes shut, knowing she'd shattered the precious moment. She regretted that, but it was necessary. He deserved her honesty in this one thing, at least.

With her eyes averted, she rolled away from him, curling in on herself. She kept her eyes firmly closed and waited for the inevitable rise of the mattress when he stood to leave. Instead, his arm dropped around her waist and pulled her roughly back against his chest.

"Do you think I'd make it that easy for you?" he grated into her ear. "Do you think I'd allow you to shut me out like this, as if what just happened meant nothing?"

He forced her over onto her back, grabbed her chin to keep her from turning her face from his burning black eyes. "Look at me," he ordered. "I have no intention of letting you off that easily. In fact, I'm going to make getting me out of your life the hardest thing you've ever tried to do. I'll have your trust, Kira. And I've got all the time in the universe to earn it."

He kissed her hard before she could protest. She didn't try to argue, couldn't bring herself to tell him how little time was left for them. She took his face in her hands and gave in to the demands of his kiss, grateful that he wouldn't see the few tears that slipped from her closed eyes, over her temples and into her hair.

CHAPTER TEN

My parents' funeral was three days ago. I still can't believe they're gone. It's not real. It can't be real. I'm so numb. I keep waiting for the truth to sink in. I don't know what I'd do without Eian. He's my support. I'm so glad I have him now.

—From the journal of Kira Farseaker

KIRA SAT up in bed when the annoying noise in her dream turned into the sound of her pocket-comm. She lurched to the side of the bed and scrambled through her robe, extracting the comm with a hissed curse.

"Kira here," she huffed into it, blinking her eyes against the bright glare of sunlight.

"Kira! Damn it, where the hell have you been? I've been trying to reach you for the last five minutes!"

"Cool off, Jo," Kira grumbled, then realized sunlight flooded her room. "What time is it anyway?"

"Ten," Jo said, her tone barely veering away from recrimination.

"What?" Kira rolled out of bed and stood. "Why didn't anyone wake me?"

"What do you think I'm doing?"

"I meant earlier."

"Kira, I didn't call you just to get your ass out of bed. We need you in Command a-sap. Something's happened."

"What—?"

"Just get here." Jo dropped her voice. "It's bad."

"There in ten. Kira out." She flicked her robe up from the floor and shrugged it on. When she turned back to the bed, David was awake and watching her.

"Serious news, I take it?"

His deep, quiet voice made her shiver, memories of the night before prodding her with every move of her pleasantly sore muscles. "Yes." She wiped all emotion from her voice, if not her mind. "I'm needed in Command."

"I'll get dressed."

He climbed out of bed, and the sight of his firm body in the morning sun made her mouth dry and her pulse pound loud in her ears.

"I'll be right back," she mumbled and escaped to her dressing room before her body could work itself to full arousal.

A short command broke the hermetic seal over the wardrobe, allowing Kira to fumble through clothing she'd had no use for in years. When she'd first sealed this closet, fashion had dictated garish, big and dramatic costumes. But feathers, sequins and metallic fabrics weren't exactly good for inspiring faith in her leadership abilities. Digging deep into the den of clothes, she found a multi-purpose forest green bodysuit.

"Perfect in a pinch," she mumbled, unearthing a black utility belt and a comfortable pair of black boots. The under-wear she'd left behind consisted of lace and silk fabrics that were generally as uncomfortable as they were pretty. But she managed to come up with a reasonably practical pair of silk briefs and a silk bra. Dressing took her less time than rummaging around had taken.

She returned to her bedroom fastening the belt. She looked up from the latch to see David staring at her, his gaze taking in the skin-hugging jumpsuit. Her pulse raced. Damn, but he was making it hard for her to concentrate on anything but getting him into bed again.

"Ready?" she asked, turning her back on him.

She left the room without waiting for his response but knew he followed. All the way to the nearest lift, she was uncomfortably aware of his gaze on her body and the back of her head. Self-consciously, she ran her fingers through her hair, working out the kinks as the lift doors opened.

They rode down in heavy silence. Kira spent the ride trying to ignore the nagging warmth of his body, so near hers, and his tantalizing scent. She kept her face focused on the lift doors, afraid that if she looked into his eyes, she would lose herself there. The need to have him again, to take and give and forget for another brief moment was like a drug she craved more than food and water. And she was terrified of that feeling. So she let the silence stretch between them until her ears rang with it.

The instant the doors opened, however, sound assaulted them. People rushed back and forth in the corridors, shouting information to each other in passing. Expressions of concern mingled with determination on each face.

This time Kira's pulse beat with the adrenaline of fear. She jerked her head for David to follow and hurried to Command, all thoughts of desire pushed aside. Jo was standing over Grainne's shoulder at the computer block, talking in her ear as the redhead worked. Before moving to Jo, Kira searched the crowded room with a glance, spotted Sam and signaled him to her.

"Sam, make sure David gets something to eat." She turned to the man in whose arms she'd spent the night. "I'll see you when I can." Then she walked away before he could protest the dismissal.

"Jo?" She stopped at her second's shoulder, studying the rows of numbers and maps Grainne was pulling up on the computer screen. "What's happened?"

Jo's violet eyes were narrowed, her dark brow creased. "Very early this morning we intercepted a coded message. The code was easy enough to break for someone of Pat's skill, but not the kind of thing the average hacker could have picked up. Anyway, the message was from Ennoren to the Lord High Senator at Avenmore, detailing the midnight capture of a living Shifter. He was requesting permission to move the Shifter to SRC for...study. He hinted that there was something unusual about this particular Shifter."

Kira's breathing came fast and hard as Jo relayed the contents of the message. It couldn't be. He couldn't have uncovered the new ones. Not now, not when they were so close to getting them off-planet. "Chrissake, Jo, why didn't anyone wake me?"

Jo exchanged a worried look with Grainne before answering. "Kira, Breeanne was on duty when the message came in and was decoded. Without…without clearing it with me first, she took a small band out to retrieve the Shifter before it could be moved from General Headquarters."

"She did what?" Kira shook with fear, worry and rage. She took a long, slow breath and nodded for Jo to continue.

"The message indicated that they'd be moving the Shifter by mid-morning. She left a log saying she didn't feel there was any time to waste. She took James, Paul and Daq…"

"Daq! Good God, what was she thinking? Going into GH after a possibly evolved Shifter with another evolved Shifter in tow? Where the hell was Pat through all this?"

"Pat hacked into GH's mainframe to get a location on the Shifter. While he was in there, he found the key he needed to get us a working clearance code. He didn't realize Breeanne intended to go without telling you until a few hours after she left. We called you as soon as we found out."

"Shit," Kira hissed. Then, because cussing helped to release the tension clenching her stomach, she let lose a string of colorful and heartfelt curses. "Is there any word from her?" she asked her second when she ran out of expletives. Again Grainne and Jo exchanged a look, and Kira felt the curses bubble up in her throat again.

"We've been trying to contact her but with no luck. And there's more."

Jo paused and Kira's gut clenched.

"While we were waiting for you to come down, we intercepted a second transmission, this one coded to the newscasters. It announced the public execution of a small band of terrorists who tried to subvert GH early this morning. To take place at sunset." Jo took a deep breath. "It also announced the simultaneous capture of a Shifter—a Shifter aiding the terrorists in their attack." Jo's voice failed her, and she looked away.

Kira's every cell seemed frozen with terror. She turned to Grainne for confirmation.

The redhead nodded. "Kira, they said they were sending Daq to Shifter Research Center. If those government scientist bastards get a hold of Daq, they're gonna have evidence of the evolved Shifters."

"What about the other one, the one that was captured last night?"

"No word. It might very well have been a hoax. We don't know yet."

Kira dropped a hand to the cold metal of the computer block, then punched it. The sound echoed in the large room and the churning noise around her fell silent. She felt the gaze of everyone in the room on her. For an instant, she wanted to cry and scream and curl into a little ball. She wanted to be ignorant and innocent again so she didn't have to make these kinds of decisions.

"Where the hell is Pat?" she grated, clenching her eyes shut.

Jo answered this time. "Working at the computer board in your office."

"Get him." Kira stood rigid and silent until the hacker joined her. "You got a clearance code yet?"

Pat smiled despite the anger radiating out of his leader.

"Bet your ass, honeycomb. I'll have it ready for use within the hour."

"That's the first good news I've heard in days." She rested a hand on his shoulder briefly, then sent him back to her office. "Where's Raf?"

"Right behind you."

His voice so close surprised her. She spun to face him. "You think you can be ready to leave by tomorrow morning, midmorning at the latest?"

He scratched his chin and chewed at his lower lip. "That'll be pushing it. But I think Sonia can have the ship to running speed by then."

"I need you to know it, Tygran. Report back in the hour. If you can't get us out by morning, I need the earliest time we can leave."

"How are you planning to get all your gear and people to the ship?"

"I'm not. You're gonna bring the ship to us."

"And where in the name of hell am I gonna land a starship near here?"

Kira laughed humorlessly. "I take it you've never seen my backyard." She walked away from the gaping pilot, signaling Jo to follow.

The silence was heavy between them as they stalked toward the Shifter's wing of the complex. Kira's gut burned but her mind ran at high speed, clear and determined. They didn't have to knock when they reached Xep's room. The door was open and the Shifter was in conference with three other Shifters. Xep looked up when Kira walked in and nodded, but didn't waste energy shifting enough to convey a human expression.

"You've heard?" Xep asked her simply.

"Just now. I take it you didn't know earlier?" There was an edge of warning in her mind voice.

"Daq left without telling any of us. Felt that the situation could be handled without sounding an alarm."

Kira snorted. *"What's the verdict?"* She nodded at the other Shifters.

All four turned multifaceted eyes on her; three of the four had the blue-green-purple shades of Xep's line. The other's eyes whirled through red to orange to yellow. Daq was of Xep's line, though Kira had never been clear who was technically older—who was the "propagator" of the other—only that they were sprung from the same line.

"We intend to help in the rescue," Rel, the Shifter with red-orange eyes, said.

"Daq is of our line," Voz, with blue-green eyes, added. *"SRC must not discover our change."*

"Agreed. And thanks for your help. Pat will have a clearance code within the hour. We'll leave tomorrow morning, if Tygran can get the ship ready by then—by afternoon at the latest. For now, I need you four down in Command so we can figure out how to break into GH. Successfully, this time."

After a moment's hesitation, she added, *"Only you four will go with us. If something goes wrong, you're all under orders to escape using any means possible. We can't have SRC discovering you. Got it? Rel, you're the most vulnerable to the detectors since you can't shift to non-organic, so I want you on special guard."*

"Yes," Rel answered, its golden head nodding in a very human affirmation.

"You've got ten to get back up to Command." She met

each of their gazes. *"I know you can't hurt humans. I wouldn't ask it of you. But bring stun blasters—and don't be afraid to use them. That's another order."*

Four golden heads nodded this time.

With a parting curt jerk of her head, Kira left the room, Jo at her side. "I'm gonna need stun blasters for all four Shifters, and multi-phase blasters for me and two other humans."

"Who?" Jo asked without looking at her.

"I'll ask for volunteers."

"May I?"

"No. I need you here."

Jo accepted the decision wordlessly, her expression never changing. They separated, Kira heading back to Command, Jo to the armory for the needed weapons.

"XEP?"

The Shifter turned at the sound of David's question. David watched as blue-green eyes whirled and the golden head tilted to one side. After a moment, a mouth formed in the face, a half shift that David found almost more disconcerting than a full shift.

"I am Voz," the Shifter replied. "You wish to speak with Xep?"

"Yeah. I need to see him."

The mouth turned up in a smile. "Follow me."

Voz turned, but not before David saw the mouth melt away. He grimaced but followed the graceful, lean form of the Shifter.

Voz led him to a room just outside Command. Three other Shifters were in the room, each holding a blaster. David stopped in the doorway, staring warily at the group. Of the three, two had the bluish eyes he associated with Xep. The third had strange red-orange eyes.

One of the blue-eyed Shifters detached from the group and joined David at the door. The Shifter's head hazed and folded and blended until the human male face that David thought of as Xep sat atop an unshifted golden body.

"That's weird," David muttered.

"The partial shifts?" Xep smiled. "I like them. They're easier to maintain," he added when David grimaced. "What do you wish to talk about?"

"You're going with Kira? To rescue the people captured?"

"How—?"

"I've got good ears. And a…persuasive personality." At the Shifter's stare, David said, "Sam told me when I asked. He actually threw it at me like a missile. Are you planning to go?"

"Yes."

"I need to go with you."

Xep's blue eyes widened. "Have you asked Kira?"

"No. You know as well as I do that she won't let me go."

"But after last night, I had hoped…"

"Xep, last night Kira and I got a lot of things out in the open, but it isn't easy for her to give her trust to me. I tried. I don't have it yet. Which means she won't trust me to go on this mission. But without my knowledge of the cellblock and the security codes, you'll never get in and out without alerting half of GH. And…"

"And?" Xep prompted.

"And I think this is a trap. For Kira. It's the type of thing Commander Ennoren would set up. He wants her, and he wants her bad, Xep."

Xep studied him in silence for a long moment. David didn't fidget, but it took an act of will.

Finally, Xep said, "Kira will think you're part of the trap. That you want to go along in order to assure that she and her people are captured."

"I know."

"That isn't true though, is it?"

"I thought you could read my mind, Xep."

The Shifter smiled. "If you allow me to, I can. But without your permission, I wouldn't. I can, however, detect certain…things, as I said before. And I don't think you're part of this particular trap—though—" Xep's tone hardened just a bit, "—I do believe you're part of another. But that's for a different time. Will you answer my question?"

"I'm not going to lead her into Ennoren's arms at GH, if that's what you want to know. I'll help you rescue your people."

"I believe you. But it's not my decision to make. It's Kira's. And as you already pointed out, it's most likely she won't allow you to go with us."

"Xep, without me—"

"There might be another way," the Shifter interrupted. "If you were to allow me into your thoughts—the pictures only. You'd have to try not to put words to those pictures, try not to condense them in that way—if you were to allow that, I could act as…translator. You could show me the correct paths and codes, and I would lead Kira."

"You want me to let you into my head? Willingly?"

The Shifter nodded.

"Will I be able to control what you have access to?"

"Mostly. But some of your errant thoughts will come to me also. You don't have the control required to keep them all to yourself."

David groaned and looked at the wall behind Xep. He knew Kira was in trouble, felt it in his bones the way he could feel trouble when he was undercover in the Docks. And he'd learned enough about Ennoren to know that this could easily be a trap for her. David wasn't sure if the Commander would kill her if he caught her, but he couldn't be certain he would let her live, either.

He also knew with unfailing certainty that Kira wouldn't trust him, or let him go along willingly. Her lack of trust dug at his gut; it surprised him to realize how much he wanted it. He couldn't blame her for not trusting him. He could expect no less from a woman like Kira, and it was one of the things he found so compelling about her. But he wanted, needed, her to give him that part of her. At the moment, however, fear for her life was his top concern. Time later for trust, he told himself, ignoring his underlying fear that there wasn't enough time left.

Without her trust, he was left with two choices. He could sneak into the group with Xep's help and deal with Kira's outrage later. That would be his first choice, except that it was clear the Shifter wasn't prepared to help him in that way. The second choice, to let Xep into his mind, left David feeling unclean and violated. He couldn't be sure what he'd reveal to the Shifter, and he still held enough secrets to fear what would happened if Xep discovered them. There were things best not unearthed just yet.

Unfortunately, unless he accepted Xep's offer to work as "translator", David had no way of helping Kira without alienating her entirely. The thought of never being allowed to touch her again, of never feeling her hands on his skin or her hair against his cheek made him shudder. And he knew then just how painful it would be to lose her. That realization surprised him more than his need for her trust. It should have felt absurd, too sudden, unfounded—but it didn't. It felt unquestionably obvious. And right. He needed more than her trust. He needed her.

"Damn it to hell," he muttered. Then looked back at Xep. "All right, golden boy, I'll agree to let you in on two conditions. One, nothing you discover goes beyond the two of us. I've got reasons for a lot of what I've done and what I'm doing, and I don't want you screwing all of it up because of some half-baked notion of loyalty." When Xep opened his mouth, David said, "In return, I can promise you I won't hurt her or allow her to be hurt. Not if I can possibly prevent it."

Slowly, the human head on the Shifter body nodded, and David continued. "Second condition, you personally guarantee me that she gets back here alive and safe. I want you watching her back, Xep. I want your guarantee that you'll keep her from letting her own notions of nobility get the best of her."

At this, Xep actually smiled. "You've my guarantee, David Cario. On both conditions."

David jerked out a nod and a mumbled, "Good." Then he faltered. "What now?" he asked, his gaze nervously darting around the room to the three Shifters still present.

Xep took his hand, and David was startled by the silky texture of Shifter skin. He'd always heard their natural skin described as slimy.

Xep led him into the room and closed the door behind him. "Now, you will relax. And I will go on a short fact-gathering journey."

CHAPTER ELEVEN

I'm not sure I should write this down, but I'm not sure how else to deal with what's happened. I...met someone. Xep has changed my life, forever. I'm finally starting to understand what my parents were trying to tell me before they were killed.

How can I face Eian after this?

—From the journal of Kira Farseaker

"DAMN IT, Xep are you sure this is the right way?" Kira's hand clenched around her blaster at the distant sound of footsteps clicking smartly against polished floors.

"Trust me," Xep answered. It had shifted into male human form. Peering around a bend in the corridor, Xep

looked like any other member of her team. But in the organic shape, the Shifter was vulnerable to detectors.

"I trust you, Xep. But the plans Grainne and Pat pulled up didn't even have this corridor on them."

"That's why no one will expect us to use it." Signaling with a sharp hand gesture, Xep led the way down the corridor to a security-sealed door.

"All right, now what?" Kira raised her eyebrows expectantly.

Xep smiled. It held up a hand and Kira watched in surprise as the hand elongated and thickened. Still grinning, Xep put this new hand against the palm check. Kira jumped to pull its hand away, reacting before she could think. Then she realized no alarms had sounded and Xep was still in one piece. She eased her arm back to her side. With its free hand, Xep punched in a sequence of numbers. Moments later, the security seal opened and the door hissed to one side.

"We're gonna have to have a talk about this later, Xep," Kira grumbled as she led the way into the cellblock. *"How did you know that seal wasn't detector-protected?"*

"Inside knowledge. Besides, since no one outside of a few select Guards knows about this entrance, no one would suspect a Shifter of getting this far."

"Inside knowledge, huh?" Kira glared over her shoulder at Xep's smug grin. Damn it, she thought irritably. Xep read David's mind. At the least! A long time ago, Xep told her Shifters didn't do that without permission. Of course David could have given Xep permission, but that didn't seem likely. Yes, she and Xep would definitely have to have a talk after this was over.

She poked her head around a second bend, spotted two

Guards and ducked back. She nodded to the Shifter changed to female human form. *"Voz, which cell set are they supposed to be in?"*

"Set ten. Two more corridors that way." Voz gestured toward the hall where the Guards were.

Damn again. She clicked her blaster manually to stun, indicated that the other two humans with her should do the same, and took a deep breath. With a nod, she spun into the opening of the hall and fired two shots. The Guards crumpled to the floor soundlessly. She hoped the sound of the blaster hadn't reached any suspicious ears.

At the next corridor, they caught a Guard by surprise when he stepped around a corner into the middle of their group. Roger, one of the humans with Kira, disabled the man with a single hand blow to the back of the neck. That, she thought as she led them down the final hall, worked much better than noisy blaster fire.

The brightly lit, spotlessly clean corridors at last opened onto the holding cells. After Xep again breached the security-coded door locks, Kira started down the long hall of magnetically sealed cells. It was as bright and clean as the other corridors. But here, the temperature was lowered so much Kira could see her breath, and the air was still and sharp in her nose.

She was tempted to curse Ennoren and his inhumanity out loud, but thought better of it. *"Xep, are we getting recorded on vid in here?"*

"Took care of it already."

Xep sounded so cocky, Kira turned to look more closely at her friend. She was met with a smirk.

Shaking her head, she turned back to checking the cells.

They found Breeanne, James and Paul in three cells near the end of the corridor. Breeanne was on her feet the instant Kira stepped into view, but Kira kept her silent with a hand signal and a frown. Xep shut off the magnetic seal on Breeanne's cell, and Kira moved up to Paul's.

Paul was a young man, in his mid-twenties, well built and physically fit under normal circumstances. Seeing him stretched out on the single bed in his prison, he didn't look like the same man. His skin—where it was unbroken—normally a light golden brown, was washed to a pale, sickly yellow. His eyes were swollen nearly closed and his dark hair was matted with blood and sweat.

Breeanne stepped up to her shoulder and whispered in her ear, "He was wounded when we were taken. And Ennoren had him in questioning for a few hours."

Kira snarled. She knew from Ennoren's own boasting what went on in questioning. "Help him," she hissed to two of her men as Xep unlocked Paul's cell.

When they'd released James, Kira looked around, frowning, then turned to Breeanne and mouthed Daq's name.

Breeanne's full lips thinned and her face drained of all color. "Daq was taken away right after they returned Paul to his cell," she whispered. "That was hours ago. We haven't seen Daq since."

Kira clenched her eyes shut and mouthed out several violent but soundless curses. She snapped her eyes open. *"Xep, can you reach Daq telepathically?"*

They'd tried to avoid that, afraid that Ennoren would have another telepath ready to "listen in" on the conversation. But she was willing to take the risk now.

Xep's human eyes unfocused, turned inward and went

blank. With a head shake, Xep refocused on her. *"I can't feel Daq. Either there's a telepathic block, or Daq isn't near enough."*

The third possibility went unsaid.

Kira wanted to curse again. Instead, she signaled the group back down the corridor toward the door through which they'd entered.

Xep stopped her with a hand on her arm. *"There's a better way out."*

She nodded for Xep to take lead, then fell to the back of the group to cover their rear. *"Xep, you think you can use a command board with that insider information you have? To find where they're keeping Daq?"*

"Maybe. But Paul is injured and slowing us down. Let's get these out first, then we'll work on recovering Daq."

Though the Shifter didn't say the words, Kira got the distinct impression of suppressed loss, and she provided the words for that impression. They'd recover Daq if Daq still lived. *"There a command board along this route?"*

After a silent pause, the Shifter said, *"Not far from where we get everyone else out of the building."*

"Good. Voz, you're in charge of getting everyone back to the complex. Once you're on the road, slow and easy."

"If we hit a blockade?"

"Tell them you've got a sick friend and you're on the way to the medical block." Kira stopped. *"Better yet, split up. A few with you, Voz, and a few with Syt. Rel, you stay in human form. Xep, give Voz the code to get out of the building."*

They came to a branching corridor and Xep indicated this was where they had to separate.

"Breeanne," Kira murmured, "we're gonna split up.

Xep and I will try to find Daq. The rest of you are to get back to the complex as fast as possible, but without breaking any laws. Half with Voz, half with Syt. No heroics," Kira warned. Breeanne's gray eyes were wide as she nodded.

Xep and Kira waited until the rest were out of sight before heading toward the nearest command board. *"Is there a quicker way out from the board, or will we have to go back the way we've come?"*

"There's another route…"

Xep's hesitation had Kira's already alert nerves jumping. *"But?"* she asked, scanning the hall with her blaster at the ready.

"It will take us right through the officers' vehicle port."

Shit. *"That doesn't sound good, Xep."*

"It's not. But chances are, we won't have the time to get all the way back to the exit the others took before someone notices either the unconscious Guards or the missing prisoners. And there's always the chance they'll detect me hunting their systems. Through the vehicle port is our quickest way out of the building and onto a road."

"All right. But while you're system hunting, if you come across schedules, take a peek and make sure we aren't trying to leave the building with every officer in the Guard."

The command board was set in a wall only ten meters from the door to the vehicle port. With every exhaled breath, Kira expected the door to whoosh open and a dozen armed Guards to walk through. She kept her back to the wall as Xep worked, scanning the corridors with ears and eyes, blaster ready. Too exposed, she thought again and again. The nearest corner was just across from the door. If someone came through that door, there would be no place for her and Xep to run.

Time ticked by and Kira's stomach clenched tighter, her nerves twitched. She tried to relax her shoulders, failed and went back to scanning the halls. "Anything?" she hissed at Xep, forgetting to use telepathy altogether.

"Almost there." Xep answered in her mind, a wordless reminder to focus on speaking telepathically. The less noise they made, the better.

"Any sign of a schedule change? We're sitting open here."

"Haven't come across anything. Don't worry, I'm almost there."

"You 'don't worry'. I plan on doing a lot of worrying until we're out of here with Daq in tow." In the next instant, Kira felt such a wash of anguished, wordless impressions from Xep she almost choked on them. *"Chrissake, Xep! What's wrong?"*

"Daq was slated for termination an hour ago."

Her limbs weakened. She leaned back against the wall, feeling like someone had reached in and pulled her guts out through her abdomen. Shit. *"Did the termination take place?"*

She was grateful for their telepathic communications at that moment, because she doubted she'd be able to speak past the rage and sadness clogging her throat.

"Log entries for that time haven't been entered yet." Xep's mind voice was now so emotionless it was chilling.

Kira dropped her head against the wall, wanting badly to pound it against the blocks until she no longer felt the slow gnawing in her gut. She wanted to shout and cry, and knew she didn't have time for either. She didn't even have time to grieve.

"Okay, Xep." She pulled away from the wall, but the Shifter interrupted her by raising a hand.

Xep's human face frowned in concentration, then it said, *"Quick, to the other corridor—I hear someone coming."*

Just before she moved, Kira also heard the footsteps echoing down the hall. They scrambled, as quietly as the polished floors would allow, to the hall directly opposite the vehicle port exit. Kira pressed her back to the wall, blaster raised and ready, ears trained to the approaching footsteps. Xep, just behind her, scanned the hall in which they were hiding.

Though her hearing wasn't as good as Xep's, she could tell that only one person approached. That was a small relief. With luck, whoever it was would walk out to the vehicle port without looking down this hall—or worse yet, turning down it. She checked to make sure her weapon was still on stun, then waited.

There was a moment of silence. And in that moment, when the footsteps had stilled but whoever it was hadn't yet come into view, Kira's breathing stopped and her pulse sped. Then the booted heels on polished floor sounded again. The instant the Guard came into view, Kira had her weapon trained on him. It took her another entire heartbeat before she realized who she was seeing. His back was to her as he prepared to leave the building. But there was no doubt of his identity.

She knew him too well.

She stepped away from the wall into the middle of the

corridor and leveled her blaster at his back. "Funny meeting you here," she growled.

He began to turn, too quickly.

"Ah, ah," she admonished. "Slow and easy. Hands in the air, where I can see them." When he hesitated, she snapped, "Do it!"

Hands up, movements careful and controlled, he turned to face her. Kira's lip curled despite her desire to keep in control. Anger and hatred boiled up in her rigid muscles and clenched jaw. When he sneered, she very nearly shot him.

"I always figured I'd find you pointing a blaster at me one of these days, Kira," Ennoren said through his smirk.

"Fuck you, Eain."

He raised an eyebrow. "How low you've sunk. Or have you always been so base?" He shrugged as if it made no difference.

Kira's hand shook once before she could contain her rage.

"I take it I'll find the cells in set ten empty?" he said when she remained silent.

"Where's Daq?" The question was ground out through the clenched wall of her teeth.

Another condescendingly raised brow. "Who?"

"The Shifter," she spat. "Where is the Shifter?"

"The Shifter? You mean the one taken with the terrorists, or the one that brought them here?" Though his voice was casual and arrogant, Kira saw his eyes darting, hunting for escape or advantage.

"Both." Her anger was so intense, it drained all tone from her voice. She sounded hollow to her own ears. Hollow, but dangerous.

"The one that brought your friends here, as you may have guessed, was a myth. A good one though, don't you think?"

When she continued to stare, making no comment, his eyes creased at the corners. He looked at her as if he'd never seen her before. That was fine by Kira.

"As for the Shifter that helped the terrorists," he continued, the arrogance in his voice dimmed, "well, I'm afraid the Lord High Senator denied my request to have it sent to Shifter Research Center, so—"

"So?" Her voice was violently quiet.

His eyes snapped to hers. "Have you ever seen the effects of hydrochloric acid on Shifters?"

Something in her face must have revealed her horror, because a short burst of laughter exploded from him, filling the echoing corridors. Kira's gun arm went slack for just a heartbeat, then she straightened it and leveled the blaster at Ennoren's chest. "Bastard."

His top lip twitched.

She manually clicked the blaster to kill, watched in satisfaction as his eyes widened in surprise. Switching to a wide stance, legs braced apart, she clutched the weapon in both hands and set her finger against the trigger button. Her eyes locked onto Ennoren's blue, hate-filled stare. She continued to stare into his eyes as she clicked the blaster back to stun and fired in the same moment.

She kept staring at him while he crumpled to the floor like a pathetic rag doll. Slowly lowering the weapon, she took one long, shaky breath and signaled Xep to open the exit door. She didn't drag her gaze away from the unconscious form of her ex-husband until she'd passed outside with Xep and the door closed behind them.

CHAPTER TWELVE

OH GOD, THE DETECTOR PLANT HAS BEEN BOMBED! SO MANY people were killed. It's all over the news. Shifter support groups are being blamed. I'm not so sure.

Eian's been put in charge of the investigation.

—From the journal of Kira Farseaker

KIRA WALKED INTO A DARK, silent bedroom that night, grateful it was closer than her room in the mansion would have been. Her body ached with fatigue and sorrow. There hadn't been time since she'd returned to the complex to mourn the loss of Daq. She'd been bombarded with questions and problems the minute she'd walked into Command, forced to come up with solutions and last-minute miracles, required to push aside her own grief for a later time.

Now she was too drained to think. Tears of exhaustion and frustration burned at the edges of her gritty eyes. Her head felt groggy and thick, as if she'd cried for hours already. But the turbulent emotions wreaking havoc on her system stayed inside, corked like a shaken bottle of carbonated water, waiting to explode.

She was halfway into her room before she thought to order the lights on. She took another two or three steps toward her fold-out sink before she realized there was someone else in the room. David sat in the only chair, a synthesized metal foldout designed for practicality over comfort. An unlit cigarette in his mouth, his arms folded across his chest, he remained motionless, waiting for her to speak. She stared at him for a long moment, her tired mind not recognizing the intrusion; then she turned back toward the sink and proceeded to wash the day from her face and hands.

From the corner of her eye, she saw him move, smelled the breath of smoke when he lit the cigarette; but she didn't face him again until she'd dried her face and hands thoroughly. Even then, she kept her face in the towel for a heartbeat longer than was necessary. When she did face him, he looked as he had when she'd first noticed him but for the smoke now curling from the glowing tip of the cigarette.

"You okay?" he asked.

"No." She was too tired to be anything but honest. She tossed the towel onto the floor and sank down on the corner of her bed. "What are you doing here?"

"I came to see you. To make sure you were…all right."

"I'm not. Xep read your thoughts." She'd expected shock, outrage. Instead, she got a quiet nod. "You knew?"

"I let him do it. I didn't want you going in blind."

Her temper flared through the haze of exhaustion. "Why the hell didn't either of you tell me about this?"

"We both knew you wouldn't trust my information."

His quiet, blunt honesty punched a pinhole in her anger. Before she realized it, her temper drained away entirely. "I'm too tired to care right now," she told him. "I'll be angry about it tomorrow."

Again, he simply nodded. Then he reached down beside the chair and picked up a small, flat flask. "Here. You look like you could use some of this."

She took the flask, unscrewed the top and sniffed. "What is it?"

"Binnean brandy. It's sweeter than the human version. Binneans have quite a sweet tooth."

"I didn't know that." She sniffed the liquor again, then took a sip. It burned down her throat and made her eyes water. But the aftertaste was so different from anything she'd tasted before, and so delicious, that she took another, larger gulp.

"Careful," David warned, though he didn't move to take the flask from her. "It's stronger than human brandy, too. Keep gulping that way, and you'll be unconscious within minutes."

"So?" But she took a smaller sip this time.

"That bad?"

"That bad."

He offered her the end of his cigarette, now half gone. She shook her head, then changed her mind and took one slow drag. "Ugh. That tastes terrible after the Binnean brandy." She grimaced and took another sip of the drink to wash the nasty taste away.

"Probably why we've never been able to get the Binneans hooked on tobacco."

She stared at him through the pleasant haze created by the brandy. "It wasn't very smart of Xep, taking your information about that secret entrance into GH. There could have been a trap waiting for us. Ennoren would have known you knew about—"

"Ennoren doesn't know I know about that entrance," he interrupted. "And Xep would have seen that sort of deception in my mind when he was roaming around."

She dropped her gaze, frowning because she couldn't argue with logic when she was so tired.

"Worry about it tomorrow, Kira," David murmured through a slight smile.

They sat in silence while David finished his cigarette and she sipped at the brandy. When he got to the bottom of his cigarette, he rose and put it out in the sink, then sat beside her on the bed. She stiffened away from him, holding the flask between them like a shield.

"I'm still supposed to be mad at you." She caught herself as she swayed to one side.

"You can be mad at me tomorrow."

He gathered her to his side, arms tightening around her when she started to pull away. After the pretense of struggle, Kira dissolved into his embrace. She pressed her face into his shoulder and took a deep breath, trying vainly to hold back tears. He gently extracted the flask from her limp hand, resealed it while still cradling her, and tossed it clattering onto the chair.

"I'm not going to cry," she said against his shoulder, ordering herself to obey that statement.

"Cry if you want to." He placed one hand against the back of her head and stroked her hair.

"I don't want to."

"You need to."

"What do you know about what I need?"

"I know what it's like to lose someone you care about."

With that one simple statement, he broke the dam of her control and she cried, long and painfully until she ran out of tears.

"Feel better?" he asked when her sobbing relaxed to sputtering, deep breaths.

"No." She rubbed roughly at her eyes and face with her hands, then with her sleeve until she'd dried away most of the moisture. "Why are you here, David?"

"I told you—to make sure you're all right." He relaxed his grip enough to let her sit up straighter, but he kept his arms around her shoulders and waist. "I figured you needed me."

"Don't be stupid," she snapped, surprising herself with the outburst.

"I won't. And you did…do need me. Who else do you have in the compound? You're their leader, right? The one they all turn to for strength and support. Who do you have to turn to for those things?"

"Myself." She pulled away from him, forcing him to drop his arms. "I don't need anyone else."

"Everyone needs a shoulder to cry on."

"I depended on my parents, and they were killed. I leaned

on Ennoren and was betrayed. I don't lean on anyone anymore."

"You just did," he pointed out.

She couldn't deny his words, though she wanted to badly. Instead, she glared, angry that she'd given so much to him without realizing it. He met her gaze, unflinching beneath her glare, until finally Kira had to turn away.

"Why did you help me today? Why did you let Xep into your mind?" She wanted to change the subject before he saw any deeper into her.

"I thought you might be walking into a trap."

"We didn't. I didn't see any signs of one. Actually, that surprised me."

He hitched up one shoulder. "Whether there was one there or not doesn't really matter, now that you're all back and safe."

"Not all of us."

He lowered his gaze and nodded.

"Why did you do it, David? Ennoren is your boss—"

"I've already told you how I feel about Ennoren," he interrupted.

"But you've been working with a team of Shifter hunters for three years now. Why would you want to protect me, of all people? One of the leaders of a Shifter rescue group. Why, when I'm holding you prisoner?"

He looked right into her eyes. "I would have thought last night answered that question."

"Last night was sex, David. Just sex."

"Was it?" He reached across the space between them and pulled her close. "Was it really?"

He held her locked against him, eyes boring into hers, waiting for an answer. But that close to him, her head dizzy from tears and Binnean brandy, his scent filling her nostrils, his warmth burning into her skin, she couldn't think enough to form an answer. Didn't know what answer to give, what answer he wanted or expected from her.

At last, she shook her head and murmured, "I don't know. I don't know anything anymore. I only know that it doesn't matter now."

"Don't," he warned. "It does matter. This—" he pressed her closer, "—matters very much. You want to know why I let Xep into my mind? Because I didn't want you hurt. Because I wanted you to get back here alive. Because no matter what I tell myself, every second that passes feels like I'm losing something vital. Like precious moments are slipping through my fingers, and there's nothing I can do to stop them. And when they're gone, I'll have lost something I don't want to lose."

He dropped his mouth close to hers, his hot breath caressing her lips and cheek.

"We always say later, Kira. I'll deal with that later. I'll make time for that later. But there isn't a later. There's only now. And I'll be damned if I'm going to let now get away this time."

His lips covered hers, his kiss strong and passionate. And devastating. Her body softened, relaxed and molded against him, absorbing his strength and heat. Answering his desire. His touch was desperate, hungrily covering every inch of her. And with each squeeze, each nip and pinch, Kira urged him for more.

Tumbling her onto her back, he rushed to get her out of her clothes, not bothering with slow seduction. Kira felt the urgency driving him in the taut muscles along his back and shoulders and knew he needed this. She was surprised to realize how much she needed it, too.

He wasn't gentle, and because she didn't want gentle she was rough in return, demanding he take as much as he gave. He left her only long enough to toss away his own clothing, then he was with her again, sucking and biting the tender skin of her nipple until she moaned with the painful pleasure. He entered her hard and fast, his first brutal thrust making her convulse with a powerful orgasm. She raked her fingernails up his back, barely heard his groans against the blinding pressure building in her with his every movement.

He buried his face in her shoulder and pounded hard into her. With each thrust, with each groan, he asked, demanded something more from her. Something that went beyond physical pleasure. Something she gave with a tear in her eye, feverishly panting his name. It was a promise logic told her she wouldn't be able to keep. But she had to give it anyway, despite logic, because her heart demanded it of her, too.

Everything around her melted away except the hard heat of David's lovemaking. All of her senses focused on him, the feel of sweat on his skin, the smell of cigarettes and soap, the scrape of evening beard stubble against her cheek. And when she felt him pulse inside her, felt his body stiffen and heard his harsh gasp, she squeezed her arms and legs tightly around him and fell into a final, rending climax of her own.

She only realized she'd fallen asleep when she came groggily back to full consciousness and found herself beneath the blanket, curled securely against David's chest. His arms were wrapped around her so firmly that she was afraid moving would wake him. She stayed still, sighed with contentment and tried to go back to sleep.

Only then did her memory reassert itself. And though she was too exhausted to stay awake for long, her mind reminded her of the promise she'd given to him. A promise she'd given in more than just spirit when the words spilled from her just before she fell asleep. The memory of her voice repeating that simple phrase followed her back to sleep.

I love you, David.

DAVID WAITED until he felt her relax again, felt her breathing slow and steady in sleep before he loosened his grip. When he'd felt her stir, he'd been afraid she would try to move away, so he tightened his hold. Now as she lay quiet, he ran a gentle hand over her back.

Did she remember what she said? Did she even realize she'd spoken aloud? God, he needed her to remember, to mean the words she'd whispered in his ear before drifting off to sleep. He needed that more than he'd needed anything in his life. He could still hear her sweet, exhausted voice murmuring, "I love you, David." And he wanted so much to believe her. He didn't want to think she was the type to idly toss that phrase around after sex.

In his heart, he knew she wasn't.

The cautious, thoughtful logic that had kept him alive for the last twelve years failed him utterly when it came to Kira. Analytically, he realized that loving her shouldn't have happened so fast, that these emotions should be a simple side effect of stress. But his intuition, his gut—which had always served him above his logic—knew without a doubt that this wasn't a passing fancy or a simple case of lust. He'd known from the beginning that Kira would be different.

Unfortunately, neither his gut nor his mind knew how to bridge the chasm placed between them by their current situation. And until he could tell her everything, until he could stop hiding his real goal from her, he knew that gap would remain. He tried not to think about what might happen after he admitted everything to her, after she discovered that he'd been using her. Discovered what he'd done before meeting her. He wanted to believe that knowing the ultimate goal of his mission would make it easier for her to forgive him as much as he wanted to believe her murmured declaration of love.

There really would be time, he lied to himself as he drifted closer to sleep. He'd make her see they should be together, that she could love and trust him. He just needed a little more time to convince her.

He fell asleep with his gut anxiously hinting that time was running out.

QUIET MUSIC ROSE, bringing Kira out of sleep. The restless movement behind her and the arm circling her waist reminded her that she wasn't alone. As gently as she could, she slid out from beneath his grasp, then manually switched the music off at the command board near her door. She crossed back to the wall next to her fold-out sink and a door leading to a small bathroom opened at her approach.

She slipped into the room, the door quietly swishing shut behind her, and turned on the shower, ordering a temperature hot enough to redden her skin. She felt surprisingly well-rested, considering the activities of the night before and the fact that they'd shared a bed made for one person. Her muscles ached just enough to remind her of their lovemaking. She stepped beneath the steaming spray of the shower, hissing in a breath as the hot water hit cool skin. When her body adjusted, she stood for several minutes simply letting the water run down the back of her head and neck, over her shoulders, relaxing the tired muscles.

Her back was to the washroom's door and her hearing blocked by the water rushing over her ears, so when she felt a brush of cold air just before the firm clasp of hands on her waist, she jumped.

"Sorry to startle you," David murmured into her ear.

His hands moved up her stomach to cover her breasts. He squeezed gently, then rolled her peaked nipples between his fingers. She dropped her head against his shoulder and moaned.

"You're forgiven," she breathed, just before his mouth covered hers.

Water pelted the top of his head, washing over their faces. David took a step backward, pulling her with him, so that the spray hit only their bodies. With his lips still locked to hers, he moved one hand from kneading her breast down her stomach to the junction between her legs. Kira convulsed against his hand, shuddering despite the heated water.

He turned her around to face him then and wrapped her in a tight embrace. A long time passed before he did anything but kiss and hold her. His mouth moved tenderly against her lips, his hands caressed her back in long, languid strokes. Though she felt his erection hard and eager against her abdomen, he didn't rush to fill her. Her own fervent need warred with the part of her that thrilled at his tender care. She wanted him inside her. She wanted him to keep holding her. But more than that, she never wanted him to let go.

And then her back was against the slick walls and her legs wrapped around his waist, his hands firm on her buttocks, guiding her down onto his erection. He matched the slow thrusts of his hips with deep strokes of his tongue inside her mouth. The contrast was dizzying. With a steady, gentle rhythm, David brought her to a climax that washed over and through her entire body with shocking strength. He released his claim to her lips only when she pulled her mouth away so she could breathe while her body trembled through orgasm. He sped his thrust briefly, then she felt him pulse inside her and he groaned, squeezing her butt as he came.

Her legs shook when he set her back on her feet. She had to brace one hand against the shower wall and one on his shoulder to keep from taking an all-too-sudden seat on the floor.

He kissed her ear and whispered, "Good morning, pretty eyes."

They finished their shower in contented silence, then dried each other with overly large, fluffy towels—the only luxury Kira continued to indulge in. They were dressing when Kira's stomach growled.

"When did you last eat?" David asked, coming up behind her and wrapping his arms around her waist.

She had to think about the answer. "I had a nutro-bar sometime yesterday. I don't remember when."

"A nutro-bar? That means an immediate trip to the canteen is in order."

Kira leaned back against his chest and closed her eyes. It would be so easy to get used to this. But their time had run out. Realizing that this was the last time she'd be able to hold him, she hugged his arms tight, memorizing the moment. Then she pulled away. "I've got too much to do this morning to go to the canteen. But don't let that stop you from getting your fill."

"What's got you so busy this morning?"

She heard the suspicion in his voice. "Lots of things," she replied, irrationally wanting to avoid the topic. She didn't know how to tell him. Especially after last night.

"Things? Would these things have to do with the breaking down of the complex?"

Her head snapped around to face him. "You know?"

"It's obvious you're taking this place apart, Kira. You're moving to a new complex?"

She couldn't meet his gaze. "Sort of. I have to go." She was standing in the open door before she stopped herself and forced herself to tell him. "You'll be released today. By this afternoon you can be on your way home, with all of this behind you."

"And if I don't want to go?"

She wasn't surprised by his response, but it made what she had to say harder. She kept her back to him when she answered. "You don't have much choice in the matter. By this afternoon, this place will be empty and completely shut down."

"And what about us? When will I be able to see you again?"

"You won't." She walked out the door.

CHAPTER THIRTEEN

I'm leaving Eian. I can't be in the same room with him now. I still can't believe he was allowed to make the executions public. I want to throw up. How can I face myself in the mirror? I used to love Eian.

—From the journal of Kira Farseaker

KIRA WAS both relieved and disappointed when David didn't follow her, didn't try to stop her or demand an explanation. She didn't want to explain—it would hurt too much. But the irrational part of her that had fallen in love with him wanted him to stop her, to tell her they would be together no matter what, that he'd fly across the galaxy to be with her. It was an old fairytale, one she'd stopped believing in after her marriage failed. Or at least, one she thought she no longer believed in. Until she met David and rediscovered hope.

Now the hope only made her heart ache more.

She went straight to Command, too heartsick to think about food. Command was eerily silent. Most of the room had been broken down. What wasn't going with them had been destroyed. Only the tapestry of Nathaniel and Brigit remained—she'd ordered it to be the last thing removed. She stood before the wall hanging, silent, staring at the golden eyes of her great-grandfather. Then she moved the tapestry aside.

She had to go by memory. She hadn't wanted to leave a discernible hint, but it only took her two tries before she found the soft patch of metal that, when pressed, opened a hidden panel just at her eye level. Kira reached inside the small hole, pulled out a leather thong on which two metal tags hung. Then she resealed the hole.

As she walked to the lifts, she tied the thong around her neck and tucked the tags beneath the high collar of her navy jumpsuit. The metal fell heavy and cold against her skin, reassuring and comforting. She took one final look at the cavern that had once been her Command room, then turned down the corridor to the lift that would take her to the back of the mansion above.

All those that were going, Shifter and human alike, stood in the glass-enclosed back porch, waiting.

Kira went to Jo's side, placing a hand on the other woman's shoulder. "We're ready?"

"We're ready."

Raf stood near enough to notice Kira's quiet arrival. He

draped an arm across her shoulders. "Well, Farseaker, this is it. You sure you want to go through with it?"

"Positive."

"I don't suppose I could talk you into just *giving* me the coordinates to where we're going?"

"You tried that already," she said through a small smile. "No. I have to navigate manually. And I'm wiping the destination coordinates from the computer when we get there, so don't start planning any sudden vacations."

He chuckled, squeezed her shoulder, then looked toward the sky. "Here she comes," he said proudly.

Moments later Kira saw the silver bird descend from the sky, growing into a ship large enough to carry her entire group, supplies and then some, but small enough to be quick and maneuverable both on- and off-planet. She'd always considered the 12KZ an odd size for a space-faring ship—too small to be considered a transport, but too big to be a personal carrier. Raf was more than happy to point out, however, that the 12KZ was the perfect size for smuggling.

The craft came to a hover in the middle of a large expanse of flat lawn in her backyard. Three landing feet descended from underneath and it dropped gently to the grass. Trees a half kilometer away swayed in the wind caused by the landing.

"Isn't she gorgeous?" Raf murmured in Kira's ear before walking out onto the lawn.

Kira followed, Jo and Pat with her. As they neared the ship, the side hatch opened and a ramp lowered to the grass. At the top of the ramp stood a woman dressed in a bright red and purple skin-hugging bodysuit. Her ebony hair was piled on top of her head in a complicated mesh of braids, twists and weaves, decorated with strings of gold and pearls. Her dark eyes scanned the surrounding lawn and even from a distance, Kira heard her appreciative whistle.

"Some spread," she called out to the approaching group, then glided down the ramp.

Closer, Kira noted the prominently placed blaster in the woman's utility belt. Multi-phase, she guessed, and probably not set on stun. The second thing she noticed was the height of the woman's boot heels. Kira would have toppled from that height and broken her ankle. The woman, however, walked as if in her bare feet. When Kira stood next to her, she realized the probable reason for the boots. Even with them, she was still no more than five foot three, half a foot shorter than Kira.

"Hey, Raf, ya shit," the woman yelled. "Who the hell owns this place, the friggin' Lord High Senator himself?"

"He lives just up the street," Kira said, trying to hide her grin.

"Sonia." Raf nodded to the woman. "This is Kira Farseaker. Kira, my co-pilot Sonia Shen-mae."

"Some place you've got here, Farseaker."

Kira dipped her head in thanks. "You've got quite a nice ship there, Sonia. The *Ebisu*, right?"

"You've got it."

"Mind if I ask what it means? Raf wouldn't tell me."

Sonia grinned. "It's the name of an ancient Earth god from Japan representing honest toil—the tradesmen's god."

Kira chuckled, bowing her head in acknowledgement of the pun.

"Where'd you find Raf, anyway? Not exactly your crowd, eh?" Sonia waggled her slim eyebrows and glanced around the estate.

"He was…recommended."

Sonia snorted. "He tried to get in your pants yet?"

Kira only hesitated a beat. "I hired Raf for his skills as a pilot. Not for sex."

"Smart woman, 'cause piloting is his only real skill, and he's still not very good at that."

"Ah, come on Sonia, you know you want my body," Raf said through a crooked grin.

"For scientific analysis only." She grinned back. "But enough of this shit. What the hell are we doing?"

"Loading up."

"Well, then, we better get a move on."

"Any sign of the Leeches before you took off?" Raf asked before Sonia could disappear into the ship.

"Nope. I hid the ship real good, Captain." She gave him a mock salute and ducked back through the hatch. A moment later, a rear ramp into the cargo bay opened.

"I like her," Pat said, grinning up at Kira and Raf.

"Watch her, hacker," Raf warned. "She bites."

Pat's grinned widened. "I sure hope so."

Despite herself, Kira chuckled. "All right, you miscreants, let's get this bird loaded so we can kiss Narava goodbye."

Loading the ship went surprisingly smoothly. Raf's crew, a mix of humans, Binneans and droids, helped Kira's people, speeding up the process immensely. By midmorning, they had finished with the technical gear. They were readying to load personal gear when David found her.

The hard coldness in his dark eyes made Kira shiver.

"We need to talk." He took her arm and pulled her off to one side of the open lawn, out of hearing range of the others.

She thought of protesting his treatment, then decided he had the right to be angry. And they did need to talk.

"When were you going to tell me you were going off-planet—permanently?" he demanded.

"Who told you?" she asked just above a whisper.

"Sam, not that it matters. Why didn't you tell me?"

"I...I didn't know how to tell you. I thought this way would be easier. That you'd look back and be grateful I was gone."

"You thought I'd be grateful?" He grabbed her shoulders and jerked her against him so that they were nose to nose. "I told you once I wasn't going to be easy for you to get rid of. Did you think I was just saying that? I don't make idle threats, Kira."

"David, I have to go. And you have to stay. There wasn't any point in discussing it."

"No point?" he breathed out incredulously. "Do you remember what you said to me last night, just before you fell asleep?"

Her gaze dropped, a wash of heat flooded her cheeks. "Yes."

"Did you mean it?" His voice was as brutally hard as his grip. When she didn't answer, he ground out, "Did you mean it, Kira?"

"I shouldn't have meant it," she said, her voice stronger this time. "I didn't want to mean it. But I did." She finally met his gaze again. "It doesn't matter now. But for what it's worth, I meant it. Still mean it, and will probably feel this way for a long time."

"Say it." His voice roughened and lowered.

"Why?"

"Say it, Kira."

"Fine. I love you. Are you happy now? Crazy as it seems, I love you. So now…" But he didn't let her finish. He cut off her words of retreat with a heart-wrenching kiss that stole all of Kira's strength. The tears she'd tried to hold back trickled down her cheeks. She wrapped her arms around his waist and kissed him for what she was afraid would be the last time.

When the kiss ended, David continued to hold her close, keeping her head tucked beneath his chin with a hand on the back of her head. "You don't have to go," he said into her hair. "You could stay. Let the rest go."

She shook her head. "Where we're going, the planet, it's…it's a family legacy. But its location is secret."

"You'll have to tell Raf the coordinates, though?"

"No. I'll navigate. Pat's already working on a bypass so I can circumvent the automatic recording system. The records will be wiped clean once we're there and Raf is safely on the right route back." She raised her face to meet his gaze. "Besides after breaking three people out of GH and shooting Ennoren, I'm a wanted person. Even if I had a choice before, I don't now." She hesitated, afraid to speak her thoughts but equally afraid not to. Finally, she rushed out the words. "You could go with us. There's room. Enough supplies. You could come."

He looked away, and she knew his answer before he spoke. She'd expected this, but she'd hoped for something different.

"Kira, I have something left to do here. I can't leave now.

I've worked for a long time to get to this point, and I have to see it through."

She pulled away, still keeping her hands on his waist but putting some space between their bodies. "Is this about Ennoren and proof of your sister's innocence?"

"Partly. There's more. A lot I haven't told you." He fell silent again.

Kira watched the debate in his eyes, the argument he was having with himself over what he should and shouldn't reveal. So much they still didn't know about each other. So much to learn, and no time left. She wanted to tell him to be honest, to tell her all there was to tell. But she hadn't been fully honest with him from the beginning. Could she expect any more or less from him?

Oh, but she wanted more. His full honesty, his complete trust. And she wanted to give her trust in return.

He had helped her when she needed it. He didn't have to let Xep into his mind, didn't have to give them secret command codes and accesses into GH so she could save her people. What else had Xep discovered about him while inside his mind? What were the secrets he was hiding? What was he even now debating about telling her?

Fate took the debate out of his hands. Pat streaked across the lawn toward them, brown eyes wide, the whites prominent against his black skin. "Kira, we just got news!"

Kira stepped out of David's arms and faced her best hacker. "Explain."

"I was monitoring the communications waves while I was fiddling with the ship's computers. Mostly standard traffic, newscasts, info relays, that sort of thing. Then, on one of the supposedly non-functioning channels, I start to hear chatter.

It's coded, and so being curious, I record it. The code was a ball-breaker, but I got it." Pat sucked in a breath. "Kira, Daq is still alive."

"What?" Kira grabbed Pat by the arms and brought his face close to hers.

"Daq is alive. Ennoren was arranging transport to SRC for the Shifter captured yesterday. Top secret. No one outside of himself and a few Guards to know. SRC was warned to keep the new acquisition quiet, too. Not even the Lord High Senator is to know about this, Kira. I mean, no one knows!"

"Except us." She dropped her hands, eyes fixed on a spot past his shoulder. She felt the cold determination in her voice spread through her body. She turned that determination on David. "Could this be a trap? After getting in yesterday, would he think us capable of hacking that code?"

"Pat, what band was it on?" David asked.

"EQT—Zone Eight."

David's black eyes caught a feral light that matched Kira's own mood. "That band is so restricted and secret that even most of the senators don't know about it," he told her. "It's Ennoren's band. Private. He uses it only when he wants the utmost secrecy. The codes he uses on that band are supposed to be unbreakable." David slid an appreciative glance at Pat, who in turn beamed with pride.

"So, you're telling me he would assume no one would be able to break this message, even if it were intercepted?" She put a hand on his shoulder to make him focus on her.

"That's what I'm telling you." They shared a long stare, understanding moving wordlessly between them.

"Pat," she said over her shoulder, not taking her gaze from David's, "you got a route in that message?"

"Just managed to open part of it, Kira. Enough to find out Daq was alive and where they were going. Give me another half hour, and I'll have the whole thing wide for you."

"Do it." With a short nod to David, she turned and headed back to the ship. She felt him a step behind her, keeping pace, the energy building in her own body radiated out of him like sun heat.

"Pat," David said, "can I get a copy of the message when you've got it fully open?"

Pat, trotting at Kira's side, raised a brow at her for confirmation. She glanced at David. His face gave nothing away, but the hungry look in his eyes decided her. She nodded her approval to Pat, who eyed them both with a strange expression, but he didn't argue with her decision.

When they reached the ship, Pat disappeared up a ramp and Kira bellowed, "Where the hell is Tygran?"

"Right here, gorgeous." The pilot stepped from beneath the ship. "What's going on?"

"Change of plans. We're not leaving immediately. As soon as the ship's loaded, I want you to take most of the crew and hide somewhere for the day."

"Reason?" Raf was all business now.

"Rescue operation. Gotta go get one of my people back."

"The dead Shifter?"

"The live Shifter. We'll rendezvous an hour after sunset, before Lonrach rises. You know the old wash, just to the east of Capital?"

"Know it well." He grinned. "Hid there once or twice in my youth."

"Well, don't hide there now. Just meet me there. And if

you're late, Tygran, you can forget about your money. Find Jo for me."

"You can be a hard woman, Farseaker," he teased, giving her a salute before heading toward the ship's rear ramp.

"You trust him?" David asked when they were alone.

"No. But I trust his greed. I'm paying him a lot for this flight. And I'll have Jo…guarantee his cooperation." She sensed David's smile.

"We can take my vehicle."

"We?" She slid a sideways glance at him.

"I'm going this time. You need me."

"And?"

He paused a beat, then said, "I need this break." He turned and looked directly at her. "It's a long story that I'll tell you when we've got a minute, but I was telling you the truth about trying to get evidence against Ennoren. I just didn't tell you how much I was searching for. Or why I was doing it."

"Your sister?"

"Only part of it." He spotted Jo striding toward them, Sam, Vettine and Breeanne on her heels, and rushed to finish. "Kira, I have to go with you. You can trust me in this."

Jo stepped up to them at that moment, but David continued to hold Kira's gaze, waiting for an answer. She jerked her head in one affirmative gesture and turned her full attention to Jo.

"Pat found out Daq is still alive," Kira said, "so we've now got a retrieval mission. Jo, I'm sending you with Raf to hide out for the rest of the day after we're finished loading. I need you to make sure he gets to the south wash just after sunset. Hold a blaster to his head if you have to." At this, her second grinned, anticipation in her violet eyes.

Kira faced the medic. "Sam, I want you with us, in case Daq needs medical treatment."

"Absolutely," the older man said.

Kira studied Vettine, her young face bright and anxious, and Breeanne, her eyes clouded with guilt. She debated only a minute before saying, "You two are with us. Find Roger. I want him along, too."

"We won't all fit in the sportster," David said.

Kira ignored Jo's sharp glare and the speculative looks from the others. "We can't take your vehicle anyway," she said, trying to keep her voice hard.

"Why?"

She grimaced. "It needs some repairs."

"What kind of repairs?"

"A whole new electronics system, and probably a whole new engine."

His lower jaw jutted out. "Why?"

"I fried it with a command override code when we were running from the Leeches."

"You fried my sportster?" He bobbed his head, absorbing the information with an air of calm that made Kira nervous. "And is there some reason you didn't use the command card in my pocket?"

"Oops." She tried to grin and failed. "You ordered the doors open by voice command," she snapped, trying to hide her guilt with anger. "How was I supposed to know you had a command card on you?"

He bobbed his head again, stared down at his feet and let

out a long, loud breath. Then he looked up. "Well, I guess we take your vehicle." He grinned.

Kira almost laughed with relief. Smiling at David, she said, "Jo, go find Xep for me. Say I need a vehicle, and that Daq is still alive. Breeanne, Vettine and Sam, get Roger and then get us some weapons. Multi-phase and back-ups. We're going in loaded this time. Tell Xep and Pat to meet me in my computer room in the mansion. The rest of you join us when you're ready. Jo, you're in charge of making sure the rest of the gear and passengers are loaded. And keep an eye on Tygran."

"On my way." Jo hesitated as if she wanted to say more, then turned and disappeared into the ship.

Kira took David's hand and pulled him toward the house. They had some maps to study. And one or two things to discuss.

CHAPTER FOURTEEN

*Thanks to Xep, I've found a way to face myself again.
I've also filed for divorce. Eian is contesting.*
If only he knew.

—From the journal of Kira Farseaker

THE COMMAND BOARD in Kira's computer room hummed to life the instant she entered and identified herself. A huge screen opposite the board brightened. At her vocal request, a map of Capital and the surrounding suburbs was displayed on the huge screen. "Go to holographic emission. Mark SRC and GH in red," she ordered. The screen cleared, and in front of it a complex, three-dimensional map of the city appeared. The two locations she requested marked became bright splotches within the blue map.

"Okay." She turned to David who was busy studying the map. "In the time we have before the rest get here, you're going to explain a few things to me."

David's face hardened for a moment, his gaze turning inward. "This is information that could get more people than just me killed, Kira."

"I won't breathe a word. I'm not too bad with secrets, you know."

His mouth stretched in a wry smile. "I've noticed." But he remained silent for a long time, staring at the holographic map displayed opposite them. "Ennoren's excesses have been suspect for a long time now," he said finally. "Until the execution of the people accused of the detector plant bombing, though, it was always assumed that his vicious tendencies were focused on Shifters."

"And so they were excusable," Kira said coldly.

"Yes." He didn't flinch at her snarl. "You have to remember most people—including a majority of the senators —believed the scientific evidence produced by SRC. They told themselves they had better things to do than worry about the way a few Shifters were killed or studied. It was all in the name of self-preservation and science.

"But after the executions, a few people began to see that Ennoren wasn't just a vicious killer of Shifters. He's a dangerous man. Unfortunately, he's got a lot of ties to a lot of highly placed people both in and out of the government. Without hard evidence of illegal activities on his part, it was virtually impossible for those suspicious of him to get near him, much less get him out of the Guard."

"And so they sent you in." Kira was beginning to think

she understood. "Because you worked undercover for most of your career."

"And because I asked for the assignment. Getting it was a struggle, actually. The senator who decided to send in an undercover agent was afraid it would be too personal for me, and that Ennoren would be suspicious of me from the start." He shrugged. "I won the arguments. It took a couple of years to earn Ennoren's trust—or at least enough of it to get the transfer to his squad approved."

"He's a careful man. I'm surprised he trusts you even now."

"I…I did a few things, things I'm not proud of but that were necessary at the time, to earn his trust." He wouldn't meet her gaze.

"You killed Shifters," she breathed, feeling dizzy. She pressed one palm onto the computer block to steady herself.

He nodded. Then he looked into her eyes. "I didn't know either. I didn't have any reason to disbelieve the SRC reports. Even the rantings of my sister never convinced me that the Shifters were anything more than dangerous mimics and chameleons. At one time, I fully believed that they were a threat to human existence. And deep down, a part of me blamed them for my sister's death."

"And now?" she asked, her voice quiet and rough.

"Now I know better. I can't regret the job I'm doing, though. And killing the Shifters was a necessary part of this mission. If I get the proof I need, I can stop Ennoren from killing any more—people and Shifters."

She turned away from him, letting her head droop, her arms hanging at her sides. "But the exterminations will still be legal," she murmured. "And there will always be someone to replace Eain. Someone just as vicious, just as scared of something he can't understand and can't control." Her heart hurt. The man she loved had killed Shifters. She dropped her head back and stared up at the ceiling.

"If I didn't think there was a chance of stopping the injustice, I wouldn't do this job. But I believe there's a chance. If I can get this one man out of a position of power, then maybe there's a chance to change other things, too."

She shrugged, not optimistic about those changes. Humans were still humans, in all their good and bad forms. And for as many good people as there might be, there were enough evil people to balance them out. "I take it getting proof against Eain has been difficult?" she asked, trying to turn her thoughts from the knowledge that the man she'd fallen in love with had killed the very creatures she was racing to save. She turned so she could see him out of the corner of her eye, but she couldn't bring herself to look directly at him.

"He's very good at covering his tracks." David leaned his hip against the computer block and stared down at his hands while he talked. "He hasn't let enough slip for me to be able to arrest him and bring a case against him. At least, not in front of me. But I've seen enough to know that he does bypass the law when it suits him."

"He takes the exterminations very personally," Kira murmured. "Considers the Shifters his nemesis. He's terrified of things he can't control, so he tries to destroy them. I fell into that category when I filed for a divorce."

David grabbed her hand and squeezed it tight. "He won't hurt you. I won't allow it."

She watched determination infuse his expression. Not

like Ennoren at all, she thought. A different kind of man entirely. It was hard for her to accept that David had killed Shifters; just thinking about it hurt. But the admission changed something between them. He didn't have to tell her that much, be that honest. He was trying to stop some of the killings. Like her, doing the best he could and accepting the consequences. He took his risks.

She wasn't proud of everything she'd done in the past. She'd made mistakes. Some she still found it hard to forgive herself for, like staying with Eain so long. Like not stopping the execution of those accused of the bombing. Could she forgive David his past? Could she love him despite what he'd done, knowing his ultimate goal was a good one? She wasn't sure. But if she could forgive David, then maybe she'd be able to forgive herself.

She smiled, a slow lifting of the lips that softened the creases in his brow; then she brought his hand to her mouth and kissed it softly. He exhaled, his breath blowing the hair from his forehead. They remained by the computer block, hands clasped, even after the others started to filter into the room.

Voz and Xep were the first to join them. Pat was the last. He handed a disk to David, and David smiled with a predator's fervor. The meeting was quick, the air charged with anxiety and hope. Pat had uncovered the route, but also the biggest problem they faced. Two identical transports had been arranged, moving along two completely different paths. Only Ennoren knew which contained the Shifter. The final bit of information that Pat managed to glean from the message was that Ennoren wouldn't be accompanying either group, as he had other business to attend to.

That bit made Kira's heart thump faster. "Damn," she muttered, staring down at her fists clenched against her thighs. "All right," she said after a minute, looking up at the group again. "I suspect his other business has to do with me. That makes me and anyone with me a walking target." She turned to the two Shifters, both of which had shifted to human form for the meeting. "Xep, I'd like to send two groups after the two different transports, and I'll want one of your line with each group." Xep agreed with a slight dip of the head and Kira continued.

"The first transport can be ambushed here the easiest." She pointed to a spot on the map. "But they'll be expecting that, so I want the first group to take the transport here." Again, she pointed to a spot on the map, this one less easy to hide and attack from, but not impossible. "The second transport has the most difficult route to ambush, which makes me think Daq is in the first. We'll need to stop that second transport, anyway. Take them here." She stabbed her finger into the hologram.

Then she turned back to her small group. "Weapons on stun. Higher only if absolutely necessary. I'd rather we didn't have to kill to get Daq back. Sam, because we don't know where Daq will be for sure, I want you with the first group. Breeanne, you'll lead the second. Take Roger with you. Vettine, you'll go with Sam."

"What about you?" Vettine asked, her voice rising a notch.

"I'm going to be playing decoy."

The room erupted into a series of protests, but Kira silenced them with a raised hand. "Ennoren is more than likely looking for me. He's probably assumed I wouldn't come back to my own house after yesterday, which is why it hasn't been raided yet. But he may be on his way here even now." She took a deep breath. "If I can distract him, it will give all of you a much better chance of saving Daq."

"How the hell are you planning to distract him?" Sam asked, his face creased with a frown.

"I might have an idea," David said quietly. He turned to Kira. "But I don't think they're going to like it." He jerked his head toward the rest of the group.

"THERE," David said, cutting off the transmission. "It's all arranged." He swiveled in the chair he'd taken before Kira's communications board and looked up at her.

"Did he believe you?" She stood at his shoulder, golden eyes narrowed and nervous. David's gut twisted with those same nerves.

"I still think this is the stupidest idea…"

"Sam," Kira warned the medic, cutting off his tirade with a hand gesture. "I've heard your objections. The decision was mine. We all take our chances." She turned back to David.

David licked his lips and met her gaze. "He believed. At least enough to be there. The rough and hasty transmission helped, I think. The idea of catching you in the act of sabotaging SRC was a little more than he could resist."

"And you don't think he'll bring more than a couple of Guards?"

"I don't think he will. I suspect he'll want all the glory for

himself. It's the way he works. He's as vain as he is dangerous. There are only a handful of men he trusts enough to take
with him on something like this." He took a deep breath
before adding, "He may not want this capture to be made…
public, either. I suspect he has plans for you, Kira. And if he
has to…bend the rules to take you, he's not going to want too
many witnesses."

Breeanne stepped closer, hands fisted at her side. "Why
should he believe Kira would willingly take you, of all
people, on this type of thing?"

They'd gone through all of the arguments earlier. David
had hedged around answering that question. He still hadn't
told Kira everything. Should he tell her now? In front of her
people? Would they agree to let her go with him if he told the
truth? He knew Ennoren. Kira was the man's weak spot. It
would only take a little encouraging to get the commander to
slip, to admit to, even boast about his ability to bend the law
to his will. Maybe push him into going too far. But David
needed Kira's cooperation to make this work. If he answered
Breeanne's question, would Kira still agree to act as bait to
his snare?

Kira startled him out of his thoughts when she answered
Breeanne's question herself. She kept her gaze on his face.
"Ennoren will believe because this is what he sent David in
here to do. He sent him to me to earn my trust, to uncover my
secrets. Didn't he?"

This last was directed at David. He hesitated only a
moment, not entirely surprised by her insight. It was one of
the things he loved about her. "He sent me to find Kira, to
earn her trust, and to arrange to have her captured in the
middle of committing an act of terrorism."

"Chrissake, Kira," Breeanne exploded. "You know this, and you're still trusting this virtual stranger with your life?"

Kira hadn't taken her gaze from his face. "I know. And I do trust him with my life."

Her lips lifted, the faintest of smiles, and David felt like his heart would burst out of his chest, it was pounding so hard.

"Kira?" Xep's quiet voice pulled her eyes from David's face.

David turned to face the Shifter too. Both Xep and the other Shifter had remained unusually quiet during the outlining and execution of David's plan. He'd expected some kind of objection—from Xep, at least.

When Xep had Kira's attention, it said, "We've been discussing this. The plan is dangerous. You will be risking your freedom and safety to decoy Ennoren from the rescue of Daq. If you're killed, you'll take the coordinates to Kierna'Rhoan with you."

"I've thought of that," she said. "I'll make sure they're left with one of your line. Jo will be able to help with the technical part of navigating. If I don't make the rendezvous tonight, you'll still be able to get away."

"I was sure you'd have a backup," Xep told her with a faint smile. "That wasn't why I spoke up. I, and two more of my line, will accompany you and David." Xep's head shook when Kira opened her mouth. "We take our chances too. And you've sacrificed more, given more than you should have to protect us and our secrets. You are as of the line. We protect our own."

David studied the Shifter in silent admiration, wondering

not for the first time how he—how any of the humans—could have believed these creatures were primitive, dangerous beasts. Xep's nobility shamed David. "It'd be wise to have backup," David told Kira, touching her arm. "But don't forget, Ennoren will have detectors. It might be better to have human backup."

"My line has ways around detectors," Xep said, just above a whisper.

His gaze shot back to the blue-eyed Shifter. Then he turned to Kira, asking without words for an explanation. She faced Xep, her head tilted to one side. A silent minute passed and Kira nodded, her golden-brown eyes turning thoughtful. She gestured to Breeanne. "Select two volunteers to go with each raiding group. Make it clear this is volunteer only. Voz and Syt will go, one with each group." To David she said, "Xep and two more of that line will go with us. But first, there's something we have to show you."

"Kira," Sam said, desperation edging his voice, "take a couple more people with you." He glared at David. "If Ennoren brings more than the two or three men he says he'll bring, you'll be in over your heads."

"I won't risk more lives than necessary. If David says there'll only be four Guards at the most with Ennoren, then I believe him. We can take out four Guards."

"I don't like this at all." Sam stepped next to her and gripped her shoulder. "It's too big a risk. We can rescue Daq without you facing Ennoren."

David watched nervously while Kira considered the medic's words. A part of him wanted her to agree with Sam. If she got on that ship with Tygran, she'd be safe from Ennoren's obsessive rage and hate. She'd also be out of David's life forever. But she would be safe, and there was some satisfaction in knowing that she would be happily living somewhere in the galaxy, out of Ennoren's reach. David could find another way to get the proof he needed to stop Ennoren.

But Kira was David's best chance at ending this thing. If she helped him now, he could put to rest a mission that had weighed on him for more than three years. And with the mission finished… He cut off that hope-filled thought before it could form. He didn't want to accept losing Kira, but he refused to fool himself into believing they had a chance at a future together. When the chance failed, he'd hurt that much more for hoping.

He stood, bracing himself for whatever decision she made.

Her golden eyes caught his gaze and held it. "If Ennoren is occupied with trying to take me, he won't be worrying about what's happening with Daq. You'll be able to get Daq and get to the *Ebisu* without the entire Guard on your butts." She smiled and turned back to Sam. "And before the first moon rises tonight, that ship will be leaving the atmosphere, clearance accepted, detector ring safely behind you, no alarms raised by Commander Ennoren. I'll see to that."

There was an edge to her voice when she said the last sentence, a quality that made David look more closely at her profile. All he saw was determination and self-assurance. He pushed aside his own uncertainty and squared his shoulders. She'd made her decision. Now it was up to him to make sure their risk paid off.

Kira exhaled. "Okay, it's about time we set things in motion. Xep, David and I will meet you in the Creek Cavern.

I'll leave it to you to choose the one you want entrusted with the destination coordinates."

Xep nodded and shifted back to its natural form before leaving with the others. Vettine, the last to leave, rushed to Kira and hugged her fiercely, whispering something in her ear before following the rest. Kira stared after her, a mixture of sadness and tenderness softening her features.

David took her hand and squeezed. "You sure you want to do this?" he asked now that she didn't have to be a leader in front of her people.

"Yes." She squeezed his hand in return. "Now I need a quick bite to eat and then there's something you need to see."

She started for the door, but David pulled her back into his arms and kissed her, deep and soft. The way she melted against him made his pulse race. He pushed her back, resisting the urge to kiss her again when she looked up at him with eyes heavy-lidded from desire.

"What was that for?" she murmured.

"I needed it," he told her. "Now let's get you some food."

DAVID HAD ONLY vague memories of the narrow cavern room where he'd first entered Kira's complex. Brief flashes of stone ceilings and a lot of people were all he could remember. That, and his first sight of the Shifters.

This time, he took in the room more closely. It didn't change the shaky images already in his mind much. It was simply a long, narrow cavern hewn from the rocks of the mountain. The floor was paved, a smooth transfer from the road outside, and a command board was set into one wall. Opposite that was a huge retractable door that split in the middle, one half going into the roof, the other into the floor. The rest was stone.

"Where'd you put my vehicle?" he asked, pacing the length of the room.

"It's out getting repaired." Kira smiled at his startled glance. "I've got a friend who's willing to do these sorts of repairs quietly and off the Guard-monitored records."

"Why are you bothering to fix it?" He strolled back toward her, taking even, measured steps.

"I broke it." She shrugged. "So I should fix it. Besides, I thought you might need it when we let you out." She watched him closing the space between them with narrowed eyes. "Unfortunately, it's not ready yet. But I'll arrange to have it left somewhere for you."

"You spend a lot of time arranging things, Kira." He stopped at arm's length.

"Someone has to."

"You don't have to arrange everything." He took one step closer, and she backed off one step.

"Who else will, if I don't?"

"Jo. Pat. Sam. You've got a compound full of capable people here."

"But I'm their leader. They depend on me to arrange things and solve things, and to make sure everything works out right."

"And when it doesn't?" He moved closer.

She retreated again. "Then they look to me to fix the mistakes. If you think I get some sort of kick out of always being in charge, you're wrong. I do it because I have to, and because I'm capable of doing it. I'd be perfectly happy to sit back and let someone else make all the decisions."

"Would you?" He pulled her into his arms, preventing her from retreating any more, and kissed her.

"David…" She pressed against his chest to put some space between them, dragging her lips from his insistent mouth. "Xep will be here any minute. We've got things to do."

"And?" he asked, eyebrows raised.

"And we don't have time for this right now."

"There's not much time left for us, period, Kira," he reminded her, stroking the back of her head. "I want to take advantage of every moment."

She stopped trying to push away, and he reclaimed her mouth. He reveled in the taste of her, the soft feel of her body pressed against his. He ran his tongue over her teeth, toyed with her tongue, tried to memorize the scent of her, the taste, everything about her. He wanted more, felt himself hardening, but knew they didn't have time. So he took what he could, enjoying her response as he held and kissed her.

They didn't break their kiss until a quiet cough interrupted them. "Sorry," Xep said. The Shifter had formed a mouth in an otherwise unshifted head, and that mouth was smiling.

David shrugged off the Shifter's amusement, but Kira's cheeks reddened. That made David grin.

"If you two are through being smug," she said primly, "there're still things that need to be done." She pulled David's arm, tugging him against one of the cavern walls and said to Xep, "I suppose this will be easiest if you just show him."

Xep nodded, stepped to the middle of the room, and shifted.

It took David a full minute to realize that he'd just witnessed the impossible. Yet again. He'd thought he'd seen a lot, learned a lot since coming here. But this… This was…

Impossible.

"How?" he muttered without looking away from the purple sportster now resting in the middle of the cavern.

"Evolution in progress," Kira murmured.

She squeezed his arm, trying to get his full attention, but David gaze kept returning to the replica of his vehicle.

"Xep's line has evolved. They can shift to non-organic forms like machines. Fully functional machines."

"Impossible," David muttered. "They're only supposed to be able to shift to organic forms. When did this happen?"

"Less than ten years ago." The answer came from Xep.

David's head swiveled to the Shifter, once again in natural form but for the mouth beneath whirling blue-green eyes.

"A few years after the perfection of detector technology. Before that, we could hide from the exterminators well enough. After the detectors, hiding became considerably more difficult.

"The change took place in some of us who were already here, in my line, and it held in all those of the line that followed. We've always been able to adapt quickly. Hiding, camouflage, was the reason we evolved the ability to shift in the first place. The invention of detectors to find us even when shifted forced another evolutionary step. As machines, metallic forms of any kind, we can't be identified with the detectors. So we can survive."

"But how come no one knows? Even Ennoren?" David found himself staring at Xep's shape with renewed awe. Could this creature really shift into a vehicle? A functioning, moving, get-inside-and-drive vehicle?

"We've worked very hard to keep this new adaptation a secret," Kira said. "That's why I'm taking them off-planet. The adaptation may appear in other lines soon. But the longer it's kept a secret, the better chance the Shifters will have at survival. If I can safely get Xep's line to a new home without their new trait being discovered, then it'll be that much longer before SRC develops some way of finding them when shifted into non-organic form."

"That doesn't help the organic-only Shifters, though. The ones you're leaving behind." His voice came out sharper than he'd intended. He wasn't trying to accuse. He was just still in shock.

"No," she whispered, "it won't help them." She took a long breath. "But I had to accept a long time ago that I wouldn't be able to save all of them. I can't get the organic Shifters off-planet. The detector rings at the launch fields prevent Shifters from being smuggled out. With Xep's line, I can get at least some Shifters to a haven and the Shifters can survive as a species. Maybe as more lines evolve—"

"Kira, don't," Xep interrupted. The quiet rebuke was touched with a compassion that made Kira drop her gaze to the ground.

And David understood. Even with all her effort, all the stress, all the responsibility that Kira took on, she still thought she was failing them. David's chest tightened at the thought of her pain, her feeling of helplessness and inadequacy. He knew those feelings too well. After his sister was killed, he'd felt that pain and helplessness like a blaster shot. Over the last three years, having to work for the man who was responsible for Tina's death and still not being able to stop him, David had grown much too familiar with that sense of inadequacy.

He hated to think of Kira doing that to herself. But he couldn't even figure out how to overcome the guilt himself, so he did the only thing he could think to do. He took her into his arms and hugged her close. "You're doing more than anyone could expect, love," he murmured into her hair. "And in the end, it *will* be something that counts."

Her shoulders rose and fell with each shaky breath. She kept her face pressed against his shoulder for a long moment. When she stood away from him, however, her eyes were dry.

"Thanks," she breathed. "Okay, Xep." Her voice rose as she turned to the Shifter. "Are the others ready?"

Xep was silent for a moment, then said, "They're on the way now, Kira."

"Good. We've got a predator to decoy."

CHAPTER FIFTEEN

I'VE LEARNED SO MUCH IN THE LAST FEW MONTHS. I CAN'T SIT on the sidelines ever again. I have to make a stand. I have to do what I can.

I've joined the fight in earnest now. I'll save as many of them as I can.

—From the journal of Kira Farseaker

KIRA TAPPED the dash of the sportster, trying to diffuse her restless energy. A questioning "feel" in her mind reminded her that the vehicle was Xep. She stopped tapping, apologized to the Shifter and readjusted herself in the seat.

She glanced over to see David grinning at her. "What?" she demanded.

"We still have time, Kira. If you don't stop fidgeting, you're going to drive Xep and me insane."

She stuck out her bottom lip and looked out the window, ignoring his chuckle. They were concealed behind a thick stand of succulent bushes and short, leafy palms, the road to SRC clearly visible beyond.

"I hate waiting," she mumbled. It wasn't so much the waiting, and she knew it. What she hated was not knowing whether Daq and the others were all right. And she wasn't real pleased with the idea of having to face Ennoren again, either. Not after the last time.

She turned in the seat again, hoping for a comfortable position. When she didn't find one, she turned the other way.

"Kira," David said, exasperated, "sit still. Undercover work takes patience."

"I'm used to doing things," she grumbled. "When there's something to be done, I do it. I don't sit around waiting to do it."

"Waiting is what being a decoy is all about." He reached over and squeezed her knee. "But I'm sure we could find a way to pass the time."

"No," she told him sternly, "and don't even consider it."

"Consider what?"

"I know what that look in your eyes means. No. Not now."

"When better?" He leaned across the seat so their faces were inches apart.

His breath was warm against her mouth. Without her permission, her gaze dropped to his lips, then flicked back to his eyes. "No," she repeated but with less conviction.

"Yes." He covered her mouth with his and silenced further refusal.

She relaxed under the tantalizing pressure of his lips, kissing him in return after a brief attempt at resistance. When he eased away, she reached for him, curling her hands in his thick hair and pulling his face back toward her.

He stopped just short of kissing her again. "What were you like as a child?" he asked. Rough fingers caressed her cheek while he studied her face and waited for her answer.

The change of subject startled her, but after a moment she said, "I was…happy. I laughed a lot. I liked people, liked talking to anyone who would talk with me."

"Did you play outdoors or indoors?"

"Both." She grinned. "I brought home enough skinned knees to worry my birth mother. I had a habit of climbing trees along the walls bordering the estate so I could talk with the neighbors. That resulted in a few irate calls to my parents. They accused me of being nosy." She opened her eyes wide and hitched one shoulder. "I never understood it."

David laughed and dropped a kiss onto her lips. "I use to love climbing trees, too. But I did it to get away from people."

"Why?"

His brow creased. "I was always more comfortable alone." He shrugged. "Obviously, I got over it."

"Obviously."

David grinned, then flicked a glance at his watch. "See, we've managed to get through a quarter of an hour without you fidgeting. That wasn't so hard, was it?"

"Is that why you're good at undercover work? Patience?"

"One of the reasons."

"You've had to be patient pursuing Eain?"

"That's one of the hardest things I've ever had to do on a job." He looked out the front window at the palms edging the road. "Maybe because this case is more personal than any other I've worked on."

Kira squeezed his forearm and kissed his cheek. "We'll get the information you need." She tried to sound more assured than she felt. She couldn't predict what Ennoren would do when he "discovered" her and David rigging a power line leading into Shifter Research Center so that it would, supposedly, cause a massive power surge, disabling the entire Center. She hadn't forgotten David's warning that Ennoren would kill him if he suspected Kira had taken him to her bed. And since then, she'd done so much more than simply take him into her bed. She'd taken David into her heart. Only two nights ago, she thought in wonder. It seemed years now. And only moments.

"If the Shifters can change to machines, why don't they shift to spaceships and fly off-planet themselves?"

Kira frowned at the question and second change of subject. It took her a moment to process what he'd asked. "They can't do without an oxygen atmosphere any more than we can," she answered finally, "without some protection. Their cells are still exposed to the environment even when they're shifted."

"Are you sure?" David moved closer, his voice dropping, his look intense. "If they could fly off-planet themselves, then there'd be no reason for you to go."

"They can't." She shook her head when he started to speak. "They can't, David." Her eyes misted. Blinking, she cleared away the threat of tears. "One already tried," she whispered. "That one died. It wasn't a death I would wish on my worst enemy."

He cupped her cheek, smoothing his thumb over her skin just beneath her eye.

She met the sorrow in his dark gaze. "Besides, Ennoren would still track me down here. Things have gone too far now. I can't stay anymore."

"I don't want to let you go," he murmured.

Her heart twisted painfully in her chest and sound caught in her throat, choking and thick. She opened her mouth to speak but closed it again, unable to voice the emotions overwhelming her.

David pulled her into the circle of his arms, nestling her head beneath his chin. They sat, holding each other until the faint whispery voice of a Shifter woke Kira from her bittersweet embrace.

"Kira," Gry said again when she didn't answer.

"Yes." She pulled back from David so she could sit up straight. She stared at the road, afraid to look into his face again.

"A Guard vehicle passed Brc two minutes ago, and has just passed me. We'll join you in a moment."

"Thanks, Gry," Kira thought. Then aloud, "They've just seen a Guard vehicle pass. Should be here any minute."

David nodded and moved back behind the wheel of the sportster. The Guard transport passed a few minutes later. It was a small vehicle. Only large enough to hold, at most, five people. Kira flicked a glance at David and smiled humorlessly.

David edged the sportster out from cover and eased it back to the road. Gry stepped from the opposite side of the road, the last traces of bird feathers folding back into the Shifter's natural skin. Brc appeared a few feet farther down the road.

Sliding into the backseat of the sportster, Gry said, *"I could only see two in the front seat. But Commander Ennoren was one of them."*

"Perfect," Kira growled. "Ennoren is in the Guard transport," she told David. "Time to set a trap." She held his gaze. "You know what you're going to do yet?"

"Not a clue until it happens." He grinned, cocky and assured. "Just kidding, pretty eyes. I've got a plan. But it's an adaptable plan."

"Gonna let me in on any of it?"

He shook his head. "I need you to react naturally. Don't worry. I won't let anything happen to you. You've got a blaster?"

"Yeah, but I don't see Eain letting me stand there without having me searched."

"You're right. He'll search you for a weapon, and I want him to find one." David looked over his shoulder into the backseat. "Brc, could you shift to a bracelet or something inconspicuous, but that Kira can wear? I need you to stay close to her hand and, if she needs you to, shift to a blaster."

The Shifter nodded its golden head, not bothering with a half-shift to speak.

"David," Kira said, "they can't kill. Brc will only be able to stun."

"Doesn't matter. I want to take Ennoren alive."

THEY EDGED up to the area where the power conduit was supposed to be, holographically disguised among the bluegrass and shrubbery circling the perimeter of SRC. Kira lifted a palm-sized portable computer and entered the code Pat had given her. The hologram winked out, leaving the power conduit exposed.

She sent out a silent word of thanks to the hacker, then set to work removing the conduit's outer casing while David set down two titanium-lined steel boxes next to her. She ignored his careful scanning of the surroundings until she'd removed the casing, exposing the multi-colored wires and a series of processor chips. Then she glanced up at him, hoping her anxiety didn't show in anything but her eyes.

The late afternoon was bright with autumn sun, and though the conduit was located in a secluded and shaded spot, Kira felt exposed. Absently, she wondered if she would have risked coming out in the middle of the day if she'd really intended to disable SRC. Probably, she thought as David handed her a bypass wire link from one of the boxes. Daytime sabotage would be unexpected.

As she began the laborious process of hooking up the bypass links, her gut clenched and twisted. She could feel Ennoren's gaze on the back of her neck. Tiny prickles danced over her flesh and along her spine, requiring every ounce of her self-control to keep from shaking. She nearly dropped one of the links and had to firm her grip and slow her breathing. David stood silently behind her, no outward sign that he was anything but an accomplice to the sabotage. She understood his distance. He could probably feel Ennoren's gaze, too.

Why isn't he stopping us? Kira thought as she finished the last bypass link. What was he waiting for? She knew he was there, knew he was watching somewhere nearby. She'd dealt with this tension before, the anxiety of facing an unpredictable opponent. But it was worse this time. So much harder to maintain her control.

A bead of sweat broke out on her forehead as she accepted a laser pen and a trap locator from David. If Ennoren didn't stop this soon, she would end up disabling SRC whether she liked it or not. She wasn't at all happy with the idea. Disabling SRC systems might have dangerous consequences, could even cost lives if the wrong systems shut down. She hadn't been working for the last four and a half years to destroy lives; she wanted to save them.

The laser pen and locator poised before the conduit, she hesitated. How much farther did David expect her to go? She moved the pen closer but couldn't bring herself to activate the laser. The faint whisper of a breeze through palm fronds and high-pitched bird trills were the only sounds in the cool afternoon. Under the earthy scent of soil and moist grass, she detected a hint of tobacco and spice from the man behind her.

"Kira?"

David's voice came quiet but insistent, urging her to continue even as it questioned her hesitancy.

Pressing her lips together, she ran the trap locator over a purple wire. When the locator remained silent, she set the tip of the laser pen against the end of the wire where it connected with a processor chip. "Try the green wire first," David breathed, his voice barely audible above the sound of the breeze and birds.

She shook inside, but her hands remained steady as she ran the locator over the green wire. When she set the pen tip against the wire's insertion point into the processor, David remained silent. Kira engaged the laser. A momentary spark whitened, then faded away. The connection between wire and processor had melted, the chip itself fused into a useless lump. She took a deep breath, held it, let it out slowly and ran the locator over another wire.

"I didn't think you'd go through with it in the end," a too-familiar voice broke the silence.

Kira spun, dropping the locator and only barely managing to hold on to the laser pen. Ennoren stepped out from the cover of the shrubs, his blue eyes glittering with a light that made Kira's breathing stop.

"I always assumed there were some limits to your excesses, dearest. But I suppose I was wrong about that, too."

Four Guards moved out from the bushes, blasters raised and trained on Kira and David. Ennoren nodded to one of the men and he stepped forward to search for weapons. The man was Kira's height, though broadly built and of a much paler complexion. He took the laser pen from her hand, tossed it to the grass beyond her reach, then looked her over, his gaze slow and assessing.

His mouth quirked up at one corner when he began patting down her legs. She focused her gaze straight ahead, trying to ignore the way the man's gloved hands lingered on her bottom and then again on her breasts. If Ennoren wanted her humiliated, he was going to have to work harder than that.

The Guard plucked her blaster from her utility belt after a thorough, and degrading, body search. He ran a detector over her, David and the equipment they'd brought with them. When finished, he took a final moment to leer at her, flicked a negligent look at David and walked back to Ennoren carrying her blaster on his palm like a present. Ennoren took the weapon, inspected it. His expression, thoughtful and indifferent, never changed as he fired the blaster, at full power, into the Guard's face.

Deafening silence followed the sound of the shot. The remaining three Guards were wide-eyed but held their positions, their own weapons never turning from Kira. Kira's lips parted with an astonished exhale. Her first reaction was a shock too deep to allow other feelings. Her second was pure, unadulterated fear.

But she wasn't afraid for herself.

Staring into Ennoren's callous blue eyes, she knew David hadn't been exaggerating about the man's willingness to kill anyone that got close to her. He didn't kill the Guard because it would hurt her, or because he felt some distorted form of chivalry. Ennoren killed the man for groping her. He killed him because he could.

She knew then that if Ennoren suspected David of so much as touching her, he wouldn't hesitate to kill him. Panic bubbled up in her throat and clenched her gut. For precious moments, she couldn't think through the haze of fear. Ennoren stepped to within arm's length before she realized he'd moved.

His still-indifferent gaze fell on David. Kira's hands fisted at her sides as she worked to maintain control against the threatening panic. If she reacted wrong now, it would cost both her and David their lives. For one tense and silent moment, Ennoren studied David. Kira didn't dare turn to see what expression he showed Ennoren. And she could read nothing in her ex-husband's eyes.

"Well?" Ennoren said at last, his emotionless stare turning amused. "Am I to assume you have more evidence, beyond this criminal act, after your days in the underground, Officer Cario?"

"Maps, command override codes, surveillance vid of the Shifters, keys to government and private communication codes." David paused. "And the location of their hidden complex. Sir."

Kira sucked in a breath. David's tone was cold and methodical. Still afraid to look at him, she barely recognized the deep voice.

Her reaction swung Ennoren's gaze back to her. The corners of his mouth edged up. Still studying her face, he asked David, "And the location of the complex?"

"Southeastern edge of Capital. Beneath the new vehicle parts factory."

"David!" She couldn't stop the outburst, couldn't keep from turning to face him. He'd just given Ennoren and three of his Guards the location to the new complex, the group that would take over after hers left. She couldn't even guess how he'd gotten the information. The location was known to only a few people and had been carefully left out of all computer logs.

He didn't flinch at her outburst. His face was set, the scar on his jaw still, his eyes focused straight ahead, his stance stiff-backed and formal. Confusion lurked at the edge of her quickly deteriorating self-control. Was this part of his plan? Or had he really just betrayed her? After everything that had been said, everything that had passed between them? She couldn't reconcile the face she stared up at now with the man that had kissed her and held her less than half an hour ago.

Ennoren's rumbling laughter pierced her, mocked her, but she couldn't look away from David's profile.

Ennoren dropped an arm across her shoulders, his hand nestled against her neck. "He's good, isn't he?" he asked in her ear, hot breath stroking her cheek. His free hand rose to her lips, lining the bottom with steady sweeps of his thumb, his eyes burning into the side of her face.

And then she saw David's scar jump, watched the brief flicker of his gaze to Ennoren's hand. Her heart thudded in her chest. She knew Ennoren could feel her pulse where his hand rested against her neck. He would assume the throbbing was caused by fear and outrage. Betrayal.

He'd be wrong.

She turned away from David, averting her eyes in what she hoped would appear a defeated gesture, and concentrated on slowing her breathing. She didn't try to hide the harsh, stuttering quality of those deep breaths, however.

"Poor Kira," Ennoren purred, moving back to the line of his men. "You know, I didn't think you'd trust him so quickly. That wasn't very bright of you, my dear. You've been able to outrun me for years. I considered you a worthy adversary." He faced them, his head cocked to one side. "Officer Cario must be very good indeed."

Kira's head snapped up at the underlying tone in his voice.

"Did he tell you about his sister?" Ennoren continued conversationally. He motioned two of the Guards to retrieve the equipment at Kira's feet and return it to the vehicle. The third kept his weapon leveled at a spot between Kira and David, as easy to fire one way as the other. "He must have mentioned Tina. That would have softened you." Ennoren nodded as if confirming something. "She was a lovely girl. Completely innocent, as it turned out. I understand they had the remains cremated." He looked directly at her. "Not enough left for a coffin."

Kira felt her knees weakening. She flexed her leg muscles in an attempt to coerce them into supporting her weight. She swallowed hard against the rage and disgust building in her. Ennoren chuckled and paced closer to the remaining Guard. The man stiffened but didn't alter his stance or his firm grip on the blaster.

"He leave that part out?" Ennoren asked. "Well, I imagine just knowing she was one of the people I executed would have earned him a place with your group. Useful bit of history. Did he mention his association with Senator Rodriguez?" He stopped just behind the remaining Guard and pursed his lips. "Rodriguez isn't all that fond of me, Kira. He thinks I take the law into my own hands too often. He isn't out here, dealing with the chaos I deal with. He doesn't understand." He shrugged. "Not that it matters now."

At her frown, he said, "You didn't hear? Senator Rodriguez was killed last night. Seems he was attacked by a band of Leeches. Just outside the Docks. That story has a familiar ring to it, doesn't it?"

Kira's knees buckled under this blow. She stumbled a step forward before regaining her balance.

Ennoren's gaze flicked briefly to David, then focused on her again. "Leeches can be very cooperative mutants when motivated. Ready with information, for a price. They refuse to handle blasters, though. Jones there," he nodded to the man he'd shot through the face, "was a better choice when I needed blaster and tracking work done. Usually good about snap decisions."

He glanced at the dead man, then back at Kira, perfectly at ease. "I suspect," he continued in that same conversational tone, as if discussing some irrelevant news item, "it will be discovered that another anti-government group was responsible for motivating the Leeches to attack Rodriguez. You know how Leeches are. They need a reason to attack if there's a chance they might get caught."

"You… You had a senator killed?" Kira choked on the words, but forced them out. She'd known for years that Ennoren was vicious and bent the law to suit his whims, but to kill a senator… He'd gone beyond what even she suspected. And if she understood his innuendo, Senator Rodriguez was the man who'd sent David into Ennoren's squad undercover. The realization was a bolt of lightning sizzling through her system, hissing the warning that David was in danger.

Ennoren raised both eyebrows in mock surprise. "Me? Would I do something like that?" He smiled. "But of course, you don't understand the complexities of my job, either. The pressures placed on me by some of the senators. I'm responsible for a lot, Kira. I keep this planet safe from the Shifters and from people like you. People who would subvert the order of things. And if a senator or two gets in my way, then it's also for the good of the planet to eliminate them."

"The Lord High Senator would never have approved…"

"That idiot!" Ennoren exploded and the Guard standing in front of him flinched. "He can't see the undercurrents ripping at his own household much less bring order to the chaos looming over an entire planet." His lips curled up in a snarl and his fists clenched. Kira watched as he lowered his head and closed his eyes, fighting for self-control.

Her gaze jumped to the laser pen lying in the grass only a few yards away. But the Guard altered the nose of his blaster so it pointed meaningfully at her chest.

"Enough," Ennoren muttered harshly, his head still bowed. "You and your entire group of alien smugglers will be taken before the High Courts, Kira." He looked up again. "Or shall I keep you out of it? I'm sure an arrangement could be reached."

Her breathing came fast and shallow as she glared at him, snarling her answer when her voice failed her.

"Very well," he hissed. "You'll die like the rest of them. And it won't be pleasant, Kira. It—"

A muffled grunt from the direction of the Guard transport stopped Ennoren midsentence. He listened a minute, then pulled Kira's blaster from its place in the front of his belt. "You," he said to the remaining Guard, "check on the others. I'll make sure these two stay where they are."

The Guard disappeared into the surrounding shrubbery. "Did you bring backups after all?" Ennoren asked, motioning vaguely with the blaster. "Shifters? Wouldn't that be an irony! But I checked the area before you arrived. If they're out there, they must have followed behind you. Very good, Kira." One side of his mouth crooked upward. "Maybe I didn't overestimate your abilities after all."

"Commander?" David's voice captured Ennoren's attention, pulling it away from Kira for a brief, blessed moment. "Was Jones the one who shot me? Outside the Docks?"

Ennoren grinned. "Of course. A brilliant piece of improvisation on the man's part. Perfect way to get you on the inside. Kira would have been a cold bitch indeed to leave you bleeding and defenseless against the Leeches." He looked back at Kira. "Has she shown you how tender and caring she can pretend to be, Officer Cario?"

When David didn't answer, Ennoren flicked him a brief, speculative glance, then focused his attention on Kira again. All three fell silent, waiting.

The Guard returned a few minutes later. He shrugged, shaking his head. "Nothing," he said. "The other two are waiting in the transport."

Ennoren stared at the man through narrowed eyes, his mouth drawn out to a thin line. "Well. Then I suppose we should be going." He met Kira's gaze. "After one final problem is eliminated."

Before Kira could react, Ennoren turned the blaster and fired.

CHAPTER SIXTEEN

Two days ago, I moved into the finished complex beneath the mansion. Today, the divorce came through.

It all felt very final. Permanent. There's no going back now. I'm committed to this new course. And it's terrifying but also freeing. I've made the right decisions.

No looking back.

No regrets.

—From the journal of Kira Farseaker

ENNOREN STARED at the young Guard for a minute after he'd fallen, a gaping hole where his chest had been. The man's dark eyes were still wide, though clouded and lifeless. Ennoren's brow creased. "Hmm," he muttered. "Perhaps I did overestimate your talents, my dear." Another shrug of indifference.

"Now." He faced Kira and David again. "I think it's time we left. I've got an anti-government complex to raid." He smiled, turned his back on them and began walking in the direction of the transport. Kira's gaze flicked to the laser pen again. She stepped forward. Ennoren turned around. Their eyes locked.

Kira felt David at her shoulder and wondered what he would do, if he had a plan. Would he allow Ennoren to take her all the way to GH? Would Ennoren even take her to General Headquarters?

"Yesterday," Ennoren said, his voice low, "I thought, for one instant, that you'd kill me. It was a shock to realize you had that in you, Kira. You've never killed anyone before, have you?"

"No."

"Would you like to now?"

Her brow furrowed. "What?"

Ennoren nodded to David. "He betrayed you. He's responsible for your capture and the future destruction of your entire group. I'd want to kill him if I were you."

"We've always been different about our approach to life, Eain." She pressed her lips together in an attempt to keep them from trembling.

"True." He paused, licked his lips, his gaze flickering over her. "What would drive you to kill, I wonder? Destroying a Shifter? That almost pushed you to that point." He looked at David. "Would killing your lover push you all the way?"

The shots were fired seconds apart, even before Kira realized Ennoren had raised his blaster. She screamed, startled as much as scared, and turned. David had gone down on one knee, his side to Ennoren, his head bowed. She dropped to her knees beside him, hands on his shoulders. "David?"

"Just my arm," he muttered.

But she heard the pain in his voice. She swung back toward Ennoren. The tree just to the left of his head had a blaster hole in it. He hadn't moved. "Why?" she growled.

"I did it for you, my dear. He betrayed you."

"You betrayed me."

"Did I? Should I turn the blaster on myself?" He chuckled.

"Damn you, Eain."

He cocked his head to one side. "Move out of the way, Kira." When she remained where she was, half blocking David, Ennoren shouted, "Move!"

"No."

"It wasn't bad enough that he was sent into my squad to spy on me, to try to stop me when what I do is for the good. But he had to have you, too. He did, didn't he? I warned him, but he seduced you anyway."

"Maybe I seduced him." Kira stood, moving fully in front of David.

"Kira," David whispered, "don't."

She ignored him, her attention entirely on her ex-husband now. Ennoren's face was contorted with rage, sharpening the already harsh angles, narrowing his eyes to slits, thinning his mouth to an imperceptible line. She never looked away. His anger lashed out at her in near-tangible waves. She faced it and prepared for what was to come.

"Do you love him?" Ennoren whispered.

"Yes."

He raised the blaster, pointing it at her chest. She lifted her chin, flexed her right forearm and lifted her arm. The bracelet circling her wrist shifted, sliding over her skin, around her fingers to her palm, solidifying into a cold block of metal. She closed her hand over the newly formed blaster. A blaster she pointed at Ennoren. He stared at the weapon, frowning.

"Either Jones didn't search you as thoroughly as he should have—and I doubt that very much—or…" His eyes widened. "No. It's not possible."

"Of course it is, Eain. Anything is possible."

"No!" He straightened his arm and fired.

Too late.

Kira watched him crumple to the ground, watched the blood that sprayed from his chest and mouth. Nothing. She stared at the body of a man that had once been her husband, and she felt nothing.

She loosened her hold on the blaster, then gently set it on the grass. Brc shifted back to its natural state, eyes whirling a wild purple. But when it turned away from the body, its eyes softened and blues and greens swirled back in with the purple. Kira, sad but understanding, met the Shifter's gaze. In the moments before she'd fired, she'd wanted Ennoren dead. With every cell in her body, she'd wanted the blaster to fire a killing blow—to keep him from revealing what he'd just discovered about the Shifters. And though it hurt, she knew Brc had wanted the same.

The line's secret was safe again.

"Kira?" David stood and Kira rushed to help him. His left forearm was bleeding, the edges blackened from the force of the blaster. His face was pale. He looked at the dead man, then to the Shifter. "Thank you," he said.

Brc bowed its head.

Crunching brush and branches swung their attention back to the shrubbery behind Ennoren's body. The two remaining Guards stepped out, looking from Ennoren to Kira, Brc and David. Kira held her breath.

"If you're smart," David said, "you'll throw out your weapons. Maybe you'll only get accessory to treason."

The Guards exchanged a brief glance. "I don't think that will be necessary." And then they shifted—Gry to natural form, Xep to natural form but for a mouth.

"The Guards?" Kira asked when the two Shifters had joined them.

"Dead," Xep confirmed.

"I'm sorry."

"Evolution in progress."

She could only nod.

Xep turned whirling eyes to the deepening blue of the sky. "We should go if we want to make the rendezvous."

"Yes." Kira secured her hold on David's waist, then led the way back to the road.

At the roadside, David stopped and turned her to face him. He held her gaze, a crease forming between his brow. He opened his mouth, closed it, swallowed audibly and tried again. "Kira… Thank you." He leaned over and kissed her gently. "Take care of yourself."

Her chest constricted and her mouth dried. She clutched his uninjured arm. "I'm not leaving you yet. You're wounded. You need help."

"You don't have time." He glanced at the sky. Red

colored the horizon. A faint, cool breeze lifted a tendril of hair from his forehead. "I've the proof I needed, for what it's worth now. It will force further investigations, at any rate. And we'll be able to access Ennoren's personal logs and records. I have you to thank for that." He reached up and cupped her cheek. "You… I thought, for a moment, you believed him."

She turned her face to his palm and kissed it. "I believed you. I trust you."

He smiled, a crooked half-smile that stretched his scar. "Xep," he said without turning away from Kira, "take care of her."

"How will you proceed?" Xep asked, golden head tilted.

"I'll use the comm-system in the Guard transport to call this in. I've got the whole thing recorded—hidden pocket-cam. Right up to the point where Ennoren shot me. The rest I'll have to relate via eyewitness account." He slid a grin to the Shifter. "Good thing I had a spare blaster in my boot, wasn't it?"

Kira heard Xep's chuckle in her mind as well as with her ears.

"Yes. A very good thing." After a pause, Xep said, "We'll wait up the road, Kira. Where no one might accidentally see the shift. Join us when you're ready."

Kira and David remained silent until they were alone. Then Kira murmured, "You could come with us now."

"I'm not finished yet. There'll be an inquiry into the situation. I'll have to be here for that."

She looked at the ground between their feet. "I know."

"I don't want to say goodbye. I don't want to think this will be the last time we see each other." He lifted her chin.

"Tell me we'll see each other again. Even if it's a fantasy. I'll believe you."

Kira sucked in her bottom lip, tasting the salt of tears. "We'll see each other again." She reached behind her neck, untied the leather thong and pulled out the two tags. "Remember the tapestry in my father's study? It's still there. A cousin will inherit the house, but I'm sure she'll let you in to see it. Show her these." She handed him the tags. "And tell her I sent you." She pressed against him, kissing him fiercely. Then she stepped away. "Come when you're ready, David Cario. I'll be waiting for you, when you find the way."

She followed after Xep, her shoulders shaking with ragged breaths, tears flowing freely down her cheeks. She was almost beyond his sight when she turned. He stood, his hand covering the wound on his arm, watching her leave.

"I love you, David," she shouted.

And then she walked away.

THE *EBISU* WAS WAITING for them. Xep shifted from the nondescript modern vehicle back to its natural state to board. The three Shifters were swept up by several of Kira's people and led to the cargo bay where they would shift to metallic storage boxes until the ship was away from Narava.

Jo waited at the hatch with the others. She studied Kira's red, puffy eyes. "You're not injured?"

"No. Daq?"

At that Jo smiled. "Safe and sound in the cargo bay. Received quite the welcome home, too." Jo's smile faltered.

"I hate to tell you this now, but you should know, Vettine was injured during the rescue. Took a blaster shot in the leg. She's all right," Jo hurried. "She's in the infirmary. Sam says she'll have to be placed in stasis for the journey, but she wouldn't let him put her under until she made sure you got back okay."

"Take me to her, please."

The ship shuddered around them as it lifted off the ground and headed toward the launch pads. The lighting was dimmed to a bluish glow in order to cut down on energy drains while flying inside a planetary atmosphere. Kira hoped it would disguise her tears and puffy face from Vettine. Though she was worried about her, Kira trusted Jo's assurances that she would be all right. But she didn't want Vettine to be worried about her as she went under stasis for the journey.

"Kira, what happened with Ennoren?"

"He's dead." Emotional exhaustion made Kira's voice bland.

Jo nodded. "And David?"

"He'll make sure the truth comes out. About Ennoren. I assume there'll be an investigation."

"The Shifters?"

"Have found a new advocate."

Jo looked sideways at Kira. Kira meet her second's gaze. Jo nodded again, and they walked the rest of the way to the infirmary in silence.

THE TRIP to Kierna'Rhoan took two weeks, ship time. Kira had the course memorized, had learned to navigate this journey from a young age so, as her father had told her, she would always have a place to go. She concentrated on navigating and talking with her people, discussing the future. Only when she tried to sleep did the days before they left encroach on her thoughts, and coffee-dark eyes haunted her dreams.

When they came out of the final jump at the edge of the Kierna'Rhoan system, the entire group gathered around external view screens, straining for a first glimpse of their new home. Kira felt her heart swell. They'd made it. Kierna'Rhoan. The legacy, the gift left to her family by Nathaniel and Brigit Farseaker. The ring-circled blue and green planet was everything she'd dreamed it would be.

The *Ebisu* entered the atmosphere at the northern hemisphere of the planet, following Kira's guidance, and landed at an ancient but serviceable landing pad at the center of a small valley. Surrounding the valley, tropical rain forest flowed over low hills and mist-covered soil. The trees stretched tall and thick toward the blue sky, towering giants of Kierna'Rhoan.

The instant the hatch opened, the ship emptied, as humans and Shifters alike swarmed into the warm, moist dawn. Sweet, heady flowers scented the air and colored the green backdrop. Unknown animals and birds filled the valley and forest with music to rival any symphony.

"It's perfect," Vettine cooed, leaning on Kira as they descended from the ship. "Beautiful and perfect."

Kira smiled. "It has its dangers," she warned as they stepped onto the cracked paving of the landing pad. "There are a few big predators in that forest, and several active lava volcanoes on this continent."

Vettine grinned. "Perfect."

They walked slowly to the edge of the landing pad, Vettine limping on her injured leg and still weak from stasis. The others were standing in the thick viridian grass, some even removing their boots to dig toes into the rich, black soil.

Xep trotted to Kira, a human mouth grinning at her. *"I think I'll get fat here,"* Xep told her, turning to survey the surroundings. *"The air is so thick with nutrients and sweet new 'flavors'. We'll have to readjust our nutrient intake."*

"I'm sure it won't hurt you to thicken your cells a little," Kira teased.

"Xep," Vettine said, "what do you think of the new home Kira's given us?"

"I think it's perfect," the Shifter answered through the human mouth.

"Told you so." Vettine's smile glowed as bright as the yellow sun just cresting the horizon, flooding the valley with light.

AS EVENING FELL over the valley, Kira stood at the landing pad to say a final farewell to Raf and Sonia. She'd entered coordinates into the navigation system to jump them back to familiar space. From there, they'd be able to go wherever whim and profit led.

Kira hugged the *Ebisu's* brash co-pilot farewell. "Do me a favor, Farseaker," Sonia said before stepping onto the ship's ramp. "Take care of that hacker. He's not so bad."

"I'll do that." Kira waved as the woman disappeared into the ship, then she turned to Raf. "Thank you."

He grinned. "Was I worth the fee?"

"Every bit of it."

Raf pulled her into a quick, tight hug, then held her by the shoulders at arm's length. He ducked his head so they were eye to eye. "Are you positive you'll be okay?"

"Yes. But…" She faltered, her breath catching.

"I should be making a stop at Narava within the next few months. I'll check on him for you."

She laughed despite the tear that slipped down her cheek.

Raf kissed the tip of her nose, then placed another soft kiss on her lips. "Take care, Kira Farseaker."

Kira stood beyond the landing pad, braced herself against the buffeting winds of the *Ebisu's* takeoff and watched as their last link with the outer galaxy left Kierna'Rhoan.

CHAPTER SEVENTEEN

I STARED AT THE TAPESTRY IN MY FATHER'S STUDY UNTIL MY EYES burned and my vision blurred. Until I was positive my dad would approve. It's the one thing I can give the Shifters. A chance at a new start.

I've promised them Kierna'Rhoan.

—From the journal of Kira Farseaker

DAVID'S HEART HAMMERED PAINFULLY. He'd waited so long for this moment, it was hard to believe he was here. Six months, Narava time, wasn't really that long, but it had felt like an eternity. Now fear kept him frozen on the edge of the landing pad. How much time had passed for her? Would she be glad to see him? Was he making the biggest mistake of his life?

He took in the towering trees of the surrounding forest, the moist air—chilly but not cold, even though it was the height of winter in this hemisphere—the cacophony of bird and animal song, the faint scent of flowers. He couldn't deny the beauty of the place. But there was only one thing on Kierna'Rhoan David needed.

"What are you waiting for?" Raf pushed David forward. "I go to all the trouble of coming to this godforsaken planet again, hand over my nav-system to yet another amateur, and you're standing there like a power-drained droid! Get going. The village should be just at the top of that ridge." Raf pointed past David's shoulder to a hill west of the landing pad. "We'll be along as soon as we unload the supplies."

David turned to the smuggler, nodded once and headed toward the ridge. As he neared the patch of forest, the deep beat of drums and high whistle of pipes reached him. Closer, he smelled smoke from a wood fire. He stepped into the edge of the forest, giving his eyes a chance to adjust to the shaded light. The music seemed to come from directly in front of him.

Under the music, he heard a laugh. A familiar, soul-rending laugh, just to his left. He followed that sound, ignoring the music. The laughter led him to a clearing, covered with short grass and dotted with yellow-bud flowers. A path of stones led through the center of the clearing, over a thin purple-blue stream, to an enormous tree.

At the foot of the tree, dressed in a soft cream dress that hugged her upper body but swung free around her legs, stood the owner of the laugh. The woman who had captured his heart. Her back was to him, but he knew her. Her amber hair was longer, the gold and few streaks of red stronger now than the brown. In one hand she carried a basket filled with an unfamiliar yellow fruit.

He froze, staring, heart racing, breath ragged. She was talking to a man David recognized from the complex on Narava. A handsome young man whose face glowed with sun-touched color, his blond hair bleached almost white. He made an extravagant hand gesture, and Kira laughed again. The kind of laugh that only one free of concern and pressure could indulge in.

The sight ripped at something deep in David. Had she forgotten him? Would she resent his appearance in her new life as a painful reminder of things better forgotten? Could he risk dimming the glow that emanated from her? He took one step away from her and couldn't go farther.

If she turned him away, he'd leave with Raf. But he had to know if what they shared was still there, if they had a future. He had to know if she still loved him.

He walked toward her and was just crossing the stream when she turned. Watching her face, he saw the instant of recognition in her golden brown eyes, the slight parting of her mouth in surprise. She soundlessly mouthed his name and dropped the basket. The young man standing with her frowned at David, then recognized him, too, and made a quiet, hasty retreat into the surrounding forest.

David stopped at arm's length from her. He ached to hold her but fear kept him distant. "Kira," he greeted her.

"You found us?" Her chest rose and fell with her quickened breath.

"I stared at the tapestry for a long time before I realized the stars were different from the ones in Narava's sky. Then the codes on the tags made sense." He pulled the tags from beneath his collar. He'd kept them on the leather thong and worn them ever since she'd given them to him. "Your great-grandparents were smart."

Her mouth inched up in a hesitant smile. "I've always thought so. How…? Who brought you?"

"Tygran. He showed up on Narava a month ago—Narava time. We had a drink and struck a deal."

"I didn't even hear the ship land," she whispered, a frown creasing her brow.

"If I'm bothering you, I can go back…"

"No!" She reached a hand out, then dropped it to her side. "I can't believe you're really here." She shook herself. "I'm sorry. You must be tired. Would you like something to eat or drink, maybe?" She pointed to the tree behind her. "My home is up there."

He looked up, surprised to see a small wooden dwelling built in the branches of the tree. It was far from a primitive construct, but it wasn't the mansion she'd grown up in either. The house appeared to be separated into several levels, built around the tree's natural curves. "How do you get up there?" he asked.

"There's a lift at the opposite side of the tree. It's a simple rope-and-pulley rig with a counterweight, but it's better than climbing stairs all the time." Her grin was huge, if still self-conscious.

"I am a little thirsty, but I wouldn't want to intrude."

"You're not."

They both fell silent, neither moving.

"I heard music when I got to the forest," David said when the tense quiet broke his nerves. "Are you celebrating?"

"They're practicing. For a concert. Vettine organized it. It's tonight."

He nodded, still uncertain how to react. He doubted his logic and even his instincts when it came to Kira. She stood so close, a vision in her cream dress, her hair brushed by the cool breeze. So close. He'd dreamed of her every night, ached for her, and now she was within arm's reach. And he didn't dare touch her.

The silence building around them was shattered suddenly by a loud call. "Kira!" Vettine burst through the woods into the clearing. "Raf's back. Did you hear?" The girl stopped short when she noticed David. "Oh. I guess you did." She smiled and inclined her head in greeting. "I won't bother you, then. I'm sure you both have catching up to do. I'll see you at the concert tonight?" she asked David, pale brows raised expectantly.

"Of course."

Her answering smile reminded David of the fairies from the tales Granny McGuire used to tell him.

"Kira, you'll be on right after Paul's solo."

"I won't miss my cue," Kira assured her. Vettine dipped her head, then left them alone again, a grin still lifting her cheeks.

"You're playing in the concert tonight?"

Her cheeks colored and she dropped her gaze. "I have a solo."

"What instrument?" Her bashful admittance dimmed his fear, and he took a step closer.

"Flute."

"I love the flute." His step put him close enough to feel

the heat radiating from her body and to smell a hint of wild-flowers in her hair.

"I didn't know you liked music," she murmured, her golden brown gaze now locked with his.

"Passionate about it, actually. Just never had the time to learn an instrument."

"I'm not very good. But I love to play."

"I'm sure you're wonderful." He reached out and cupped her cheek without thinking. Her skin was soft and supple beneath his rough fingertips.

"David…"

"Before you say anything," he interrupted, rushing to say what he needed to. "I have something I have to tell you."

"The Shifters?" Her eyes widened. "Are they all right? Is the new complex still working? What happened?"

The tumble of her questions and the panic in her eyes pushed him to answer. "The Shifters are fine in general. Congress has reconvened to 're-examine the necessity and ethics of the exterminations'. It might be years before they make the killing of Shifters illegal, but at least the hunt has been called off for the moment. But…Kira most people are still afraid of the Shifters. There's a long way to go."

"Have they discovered the truth about Xep's line?"

He shook his head, moving his hand from her cheek to the curve between her neck and shoulder. "That adaptation is still secret. So is the location of your group's complex."

She smiled and let out a slow breath.

"How is Xep's line doing here?"

"They love it. Half of them are letting themselves get fat." She let out a slight laugh, then turned more serious.

"This is the first time in a long while they've been able to relax and just live. It's agreeing with them."

"I'm glad."

"And you? What happened with you?"

"I got what I wanted. My sister's name has been cleared, along with the others who were executed. The matter is still under investigation, though. There's no clear evidence to indicate who set the bomb. Suspicions have turned toward Ennoren. I'm afraid he took the brunt of the blame for…well, for everything that's being unearthed. There were others involved, highly placed people in the government. But Ennoren can't identify them now, and a lot of senators are more than willing to let the issue die with him."

"I'm sorry," Kira said, her eyes wide.

"Why?"

"Because we stopped one man, but so many more got away."

"They're for someone else to catch. I did my part. You did yours." His hand slid behind her neck and his fingers twined in her hair. "But none of that is what I flew all the way here to tell you."

"Oh? What, then?"

"I forgot to say this before you left. I didn't want it to remain unsaid." He dropped his hand back to his side and sucked in a lungful of air. "I love you, Kira. I need you to know that. I realize that, after all this time, you may not feel the same about me anymore. I was afraid I wouldn't feel the same once I got here, either. And I was right. I don't feel the same. Seeing you again, I realize I love you so much more than I thought I did."

She let loose a small sigh and swayed back from him.

Then she cupped his face in her hands and kissed him. David's world erupted into color and song. He wrapped his arms around her waist, pulling her against him so fiercely she gasped. But he couldn't relax his grip just yet. He poured all the passion and longing and love that swelled in his chest into their kiss, trembling with the strength of it.

"You'll stay?" she breathed into his mouth in between kisses. "You won't mind living here, isolated from the rest of the galaxy?"

"I have all I want in the universe right here in my arms." And then he kissed her again.

Thank you for reading PROMISE
(The Naravan Chronicles 1).
If you've enjoyed this book, please continue reading for
an excerpt from the next story, INTERFACE.

CHAPTER ONE

Gina paused just outside the door of her father's private office when she heard strange voices from inside and listened to make sure she wasn't interrupting an important meeting. The door was cracked an inch, not enough to see into the room but enough to hear the conversation.

A conversation she couldn't believe she was hearing. She dug ruts in her palms with her nails as she tried to contain her temper.

"Gina won't like this," her father said. "Getting her to agree to added security is never easy, but this…" His voice dropped. "She doesn't know about the threats. I didn't want to tell her everything."

"Is that wise?" a male voice asked.

"No. Not with her temper. But she'll just have to understand. I won't take any chances now. Not after that last message."

You won't take any chances? Gina sucked in a breath through her teeth. *This is my research.*

"Do you have any idea who the outside source is, Mr. Xanacovich?" another male voice asked.

"I can't imagine who would do something like this."

"With Xanac Corp's ties to the initial development of detectors," the first man said, "it could be a Shifter terrorist group."

Gina sucked in a silent breath. Shifters were an alien species of shape shifters native to Narava, and detectors were the only way to identify them when they weren't in their natural forms. She still had mixed feelings about the part her family's company had played in the development of detectors. Their research had led to a number of advances, including a way to scan for a Naravan-based blood virus that had killed many Naravan's over the years. But the DNA based scanning technique had also greatly advanced the development of detectors. While this meant Shifters couldn't just *be* anywhere they wanted without humans knowing, it also meant they couldn't hide from human fear.

According to government research, though in her opinion "research" was a very loose term for what they did at Shifter Research Center, Shifters were a dangerous, parasitic animal likely to wipe out the human population on Narava if not countered. Silly idea since humans had lived on Narava for fifty years before even knowing the Shifters existed. And even if they could potentially be dangerous to humans, the only species currently on the verge of being wiped out were the Shifters. The illogic of SRC's arguments kept Gina from believing most of what they said, and she felt for the Shifters, being driven so close to extinction because of bad science.

Still, a huge portion of the population agreed with SRC. Most people were terrified knowing a Shifter could be in their home or next to them on the street without them knowing. So Shifter exterminations had been legally sanctioned.

But not everyone agreed with the government's actions. A few small pockets of humans advocated an end to the exterminations and were brave enough to come out publicly in support of ending the slaughter, even knowing it was dangerous to take that stance. She hadn't mustered up the courage yet, but she admired those who had.

Rumors had been flying over the last two weeks about the findings of an undercover Guard concerning Shifters and one of the Shifter support groups. Each side of the volatile argument assumed the Guard's report would support their view—either to continue the exterminations or to end them. She was hoping for the latter.

"Xanac Corp.'s contribution to the development of detectors was minimal, and before my tenure as CEO. Why hit our R&D team now?" Her father's voice was quiet, strained.

"To highlight their cause?" the first unfamiliar voice said. "To move interest away from this the rumored Guard report to a topic more immediate?"

Despite her growing anger at being left out of this important conversation, a conversation involving her research team, Gina found the timber of the stranger's voice flowing like heady liquor through her blood stream. Whoever he was, she could listen to him talk for hours. He had the kind of deep, rhythmic voice that reminded her of dark nights, tangled, sweaty sheets, and murmured desires.

"That situation only started two weeks ago," her father

said, referring to the undercover Guard. "I've been getting threats for a month."

"The threats are to get you to stop the work, so…something directly to do with the research then? And how it relates to the Shifters?"

Gina's eyes widened. Had her father told the two men *everything* about her work? She ground her teeth together.

"No. This wasn't done by anyone supporting the Shifters," her father said, closing the subject with that obstinate there-will-be-no-further-discussion tone that drove Gina nuts.

There was a pause, the silence heavy. She felt a vein throbbing in her temple. She tried relaxing her clenched fists. *Calm, Gina. Just stay calm.*

"Under the circumstances, it's best if the regular security staff don't know about you," her father said, his voice authoritative but rushed.

"We understand, Mr. Xanacovich," the first man said. "Discretion's our specialty."

Discretion? This was what her father called discretion? Hiring perfect strangers then telling them about her work? Keeping threats to her research a secret? She struggled to contain a string of Deven curses. She always turned to her mother's native language when Naravan or Trade curses weren't strong enough. She took a deep breath, let it out slowly, and tried one last time to reign in her legendary temper. This wasn't the first time her father had gone behind her back to protect her. It was, however, the first time he'd kept the reason for his actions a secret.

She rolled her shoulders and focused on keeping her breathing steady. She would just walk quietly into the room, ask in a reasonable manner what her father was doing keeping these threats a secret from her. She could be calm and controlled when the situation called for it.

Unfortunately, this wasn't one of those times.

She slammed the office door against the wall with enough force that it echoed as she stomped into the office.

"What the hell's going on, Dad?"

Hands planted on hips, she took in her father's two guests with a scowl. The one standing was tall and muscular, his long black hair pulled back in a low tail showing a face so handsomely chiseled it was almost unreal. His hazel eyes narrowed at the intrusion. She flashed him a narrow-eyed look in return and got a raised brow in response.

The other man sat in a chair in front of her father's desk. She met a pair of deep blue eyes, and it took her a moment to remember to scowl. *He* wasn't too handsome, not by a long shot. But he was very male. Tawny hair, strong features, wide shoulders, a heart-stopping mouth. A shiver of electricity skittered up her spine as her gaze locked on that mouth.

He's the one with the sexy voice, she thought before she could stop herself, and her stomach muscles tightened in anticipation of hearing him speak through those deliciously captivating lips.

With a disgusted grunt, she pushed the physical reaction aside, calling up her anger. Now was not the time to worry about the faint smile curving the man's tempting mouth, or her suspicion that he knew exactly what she'd been thinking.

"Well?" she directed her ire toward her father.

"Gina." He straightened in his seat, emphasizing his height the way he did when he was nervous. "What are you doing here? I thought you'd still be at the labs."

"Obviously. But I'm not the one who needs to answer questions. Why didn't you tell me you were receiving threatening messages?"

"I didn't want you to worry." Her father raised his hands, palms out, trying to placate. Gina wasn't in the mood.

"Worry me? I'm not worried! I'm pissed off. How dare anybody threaten you to get me to call off this research? You can just tell whoever it is to forget it. They think they can hurt me? I dare them to try."

She didn't miss that interesting mouth trying to suppress a grin. She just chose to ignore it.

"Honey, you don't understand. These aren't nice men we're dealing with here. You can't possibly—"

"And why not? I bet I've got as much hand-to-hand training as these two thugs you're hiring."

"It's not a matter of training. Self-defense classes are not the same—"

"Self-defense classes? I'm a black belt in karate. I can handle myself, and you well know it."

"All the training in the world can't stop an unexpected blaster shot from ripping through you." The deep, slightly amused comment came from the seated man. And she'd been right. His voice eased through her, tingling across her nerves, and settling into her bones. That voice could conquer worlds. But his comment spiked her already raging temper.

Gina turned her anger on him, but before she could launch into a satisfying tirade, her father spoke.

"I don't care how much training you've had or how well you think you can take care of yourself," he said. "That has nothing to do with this situation. Haven't you noticed, damn it? You're one of the brightest women I know, and you haven't figured out yet that the others were not accidents?"

Not accidents? "What do you…" She stopped. For a moment, all she could do was stare at her father, anger dissipating beneath the shock of facts. Jesus, how could she have missed it? The rash of accidents in the last month, the injuries, the deaths…Two of the original group, the only other two besides her and Jack Nevel who'd actually participated in the experiment, were dead. But Mira and Barry had died in a public link accident that killed fifteen people. The other accidents… Serious injuries, property damage… All members of her research team directly connected to the experiment.

Gina's stomach flipped. It couldn't be. She had to be wrong. There was no way the accidents could be anything other than an unfortunate set of coincidences. "What makes you think they weren't accidents?" she demanded, not willing to believe without proof.

Her father sighed and signaled to the seated man. "Mr. Alexander."

Gina watched warily as the man rose and handed her a messaging pad. She stared at the fist-sized screen, looked up at her father then pressed the pad to activate the recall. Five messages scrolled past, each one more graphic and threatening, each one very specific in relating the details of the events of the last month. They left no room for argument. Someone was attacking her team. As she numbly read the final letter, she realized it detailed first the death of Jack, then her own death. She swallowed hard and handed the pad back to the still looming Mr. Alexander.

"Jack?" Her voice echoed, hollow in her own ears.

"His body was found yesterday evening."

Gina looked up into Mr. Alexander's blue eyes without really seeing him. "And the M-SIDs?" She directed the question toward her father while still staring at the mercenary.

"There's every reason to believe they disassembled when whoever's doing this tried to extract them," her father said.

"What reason?"

"The…the blood found with Jack's… The blood contained traces of the magnesium-iron-eltranium alloy released when the M-SIDs broke down." Her father fell silent, then whispered, "Gina, Jack was tortured before they attempted to extract the micro-scanners."

Gina's world tilted sideways.

**Don't miss the next romantic science fiction adventure in
The Naravan Chronicles Series
INTERFACE (The Naravan Chronicles 2)**

ABOUT THE AUTHOR

Isabo Kelly is the award-winning author of numerous science fiction, fantasy, and paranormal romances. She also writes best-selling paranormal romance under the name Kat Simons. Her life has taken her from Las Vegas to Hawaii, where she got her BA in Zoology, back to Vegas where she looked after sharks, then on to Germany and Ireland where she got her Ph.D. in Animal Behavior. Now Isabo focuses on writing. She lives in New York with her Irish husband and two beautiful boys, working as a full time writer and stay-at-home mom.

Don't miss out on new releases from Isabo! Sign up for her Newsletter here: http://eepurl.com/caxHa9

For more on Isabo and her books:
Website: http://www.isabokelly.com
Facebook: http://www.facebook.com/IsaboKelly
Twitter: https://www.twitter.com/IsaboKelly

The Naravan Chronicles

Promise

Interface

Secret

Paradise

Flight

New York Empires Anthologies

Going All In

Icing The Puck

Fire and Tears Series

Brightarrow Burning

Darkness Singed

Dawn Ignited

Fate's Hand Series

Thief's Desire

Destiny's Seduction

Kellyn's Sacrifice

The Last Guardian

Bonfire Night

www.ingramcontent.com/pod-product-compliance
Lightning Source LLC
Chambersburg PA
CBHW060543190726
48283CB00003B/851